THE
Face OF
God

THE
Face
OF
God

BRIAN RAY BREWER

Library of Congress Control Number: 2021910479

HARDBACK: 978-1-955347-88-4
PAPERBACK: 978-1-955347-87-7
EBOOK: 978-1-955347-89-1

Ordering Information:

For orders and inquiries, please contact:
1-888-404-1388
www.goldtouchpress.com
book.orders@goldtouchpress.com

Printed in the United States of America

Dedication

For God

In Memory of Marilyn, Jerry, Berton and
Wanda Brewer and Joevah de Souza

And for
Silviane,
Always.

Acknowledgement

Cover art:
"The Baptism of Christ," by Carlos Araujo, oil on wood,
from the author's personal collection.

Chapter One

I T WAS A GALA night! The bright display lighting glared down upon the mass of sculpture strewn about the gallery and flashed upon the gleaming white shirts of tuxedoed waiters as they whisked by with their cargoes of sparkling champagnes and waters. Strange, discordant melodies wove among the crowds that clustered around the grotesques they were admiring—strange music, new music, hacked forth from violin and cello in a frenzied sawing from the thin arms of a wild-eyed quartet whose sounds and appearance evoked visions of demon lumberjacks ripping through bark for the heart of a forest. Their strings whined. Their bows moaned. Their agonies screamed to the ceiling, then fell in heavy strains upon the gallery patrons roaming pensively below.

The crowds hunkered down under the assault of light and noise, some chatting among themselves and some quietly sipping their poison, lost in frowning thought—all silently searching for meaning in the monstrosities leering out at them, and all coming up empty.

The showroom was inhabited by mannequins, dozens of mannequins, mannequins in chains, mannequins in leathers, mannequins wildly screaming silent pleas to an indifferent god as they were tortured by other smiling, sadistic mannequins in methods unknown to the Grand Inquisitor himself. Other mannequins rolled the floor in stiff-limbed displays of ecstasy and carnal wonder. There were beasts and whips and chains and children. There were lawn implements, bathroom fixtures, home appliances and industrial machines. Every conceivable tool of this age and many of the past were engaged in invoking pain, pleasure or both from the mannequins condemned to suffer their use.

Plastic dogs gnawed rubber flesh. Painted blood stained the floor as it dripped from whips wielded by preformed hands to pool in crimson, acrylic puddles. Electrodes hummed. Ripsaws ripped. Faucets steamed into tubs of boiling mannequin babies. It was a Bosch painting come to life. It was a department store gone mad.

"Where is he?" asked Deborah Mondain, an aging heiress and socialite who was a patron of the arts and artists extraordinaire. "I've just got to talk to him about this piece. It speaks to me like nothing else he's done before!"

She gazed at the mannequin above, arched backward to the sky, whose painted eyes shone in ecstasy as it pulled at the safety pin piercing its breast and gently massaged the railroad tie that skewered and thrust it toward the ceiling. Chemical blood ran down its fiberglass fingers, touching the railroad tie and slowly dripping from its elbow to an expectant crowd of plastic rats that were mechanically scratching and squeaking below.

"He hasn't yet made his appearance, Deborah," soothed Armine Quadras, the gallery owner. "But when he does arrive, I'll be sure he sees you. It's outrageous isn't it?" She gazed up with her hands pressed together as if in prayer.

Deborah sighed and nodded her assent. Patrons gathered around the two and joined their reverie, while others milled about the different exhibits, drinking and talking and secretly wondering why they couldn't seem to appreciate this razor's edge display of contemporary art.

The gallery doors burst open, and with a rush of cold air and a whirl of snowflakes, entered the artist. Cameras flashed and whirred as society reporters and art critics fell in behind him as he strode to the center of the gallery floor. Armine moved to meet him. They kissed each other lightly on the cheek, and a brief glimmer flashed between their eyes. Her hand on his elbow, they spun to face the crowd.

"Ladies and gentlemen, I present to you the man whose vision and struggle has captured for you, and for the world, this subtle glimpse of a greater reality. Tonight, you have the honor of being presented with this artist's work."

Applause thundered. Cameras flashed again.

"Ladies and gentlemen," she sounded, "I give you Martin Drake!"

He bowed deeply and then bowed once more, a Shakespearean at the close of a play. Martin stood tall in a dark suit and a black Nehru shirt, gazing out at the admiring crowd with dark, piercing eyes that could have belonged to a prophet. He swept a shock of chestnut hair back from his handsome forehead, then raised his hand, set his face with a proper mix of pride and humility, and said in an almost musical tenor, "Thank you! Thank you all. I hope that you have found these musings of mine to be of meaning. Enjoy the drink. Enjoy the food. Enjoy the art as much as I enjoy your thoughtful presence here tonight. Thank you!"

With a deft hand, he slipped a glass of whiskey off the tray of a nearby waiter and downed it in an instant. He traded that glass for another, then dove into the sea of outstretched hands and glistening smiles lapping toward him like waves.

"Marvelous, Martin, just marvelous! Once again you've managed to shock this callused critic," said a squat, red-faced man before him.

Callused around the bunghole maybe, you disgusting old fag, thought Martin as he took the critic's hand and smiled.

"Why thank you, Peter," said Martin. "It's always good to hear praise from a discerning man. I hope you'll have something nice to say about my exhibition in *The Times*."

"I certainly will! These pieces, the way you've styled them, it shows a new current that is sure to ripple throughout the art world. Your use and abuse of these mannequins subtly suggests an even darker side of your work." The red-faced man hesitated for a moment before rushing on. "And, well…honestly, a trace of homoeroticism that you had until now suppressed in your work."

Martin feigned shock and thought, *I'd like to suppress you, you pompous slug. You could find a trace of homoeroticism in an ashtray if you could manage to cram it up your ass.* Instead he said, "Peter, I'm flattered that you think this work is important, but as to its content? I always leave that to the viewer."

A hand lit on his shoulder. He smiled at the critic then turned to face the mayor's assistant for culture and the arts, Kimble Gentry. *God, another one*, he thought.

"Hello, Kimble, how's the battle at city hall? Come by to commission me to bronze the mayor?"

"No, Martin, I'm afraid that not even this mayor is foolish enough to spend city money on a statue of himself in these hard times," said Kimble, who then smirked. "Although I imagine that the thought has crossed his mind."

"Well, why don't you knock down the Saint-Gaudens on top of Grand Central Station and install a few of these?" Martin waved a hand toward the horrors that surrounded them.

"Switching those old statues for some of your mannequins…the idea sounds intriguing," he said, placing a finger to his lips in contemplation.

It would intrigue you, Tinkerbell, thought Martin. "Just say when, Kimble, and I'll weatherize them and ship them right out to you, and if the mayor ever does decide to immortalize himself, talk me up. I don't know if I can do a better job than the political cartoonists, but at least I can make him larger than life—the sky's the limit!"

Martin drained his second whiskey. "In the meantime, why don't you acquire some of my work for one of the museums. Look around, Kimble. Can you afford to miss this?"

"I know that we should stay current, but to be honest, our funding isn't what it was," he said. "Quite frankly, I'm not sure that we can afford you anymore."

"Well, look around, look around, and if you see anything that strikes you, I'll ask Armine to go easy. I've always been a believer in supporting our museums. Good for business."

Martin winked and raised his glass to take another drink but found it empty. He motioned to a waiter for a refill.

"That's wonderful of you, Martin," Kimble said. "Anything here would be a welcome addition."

To what, he wondered, *a department store for sadists?*

"Well, look around and enjoy yourself, Kimble."

Martin patted Kimble on the shoulder and moved off. He worked his way through the crowd, shaking hands and trading inanities with his patrons, paying special attention to former buyers of his work and to anyone he hadn't met but who was currently in the society section. He was talking to Mary Beth Winston, a client who had collected many of his smaller works in steel, when he saw his agent Armine waving to him from across the gallery. Martin excused himself and moved slowly toward her, smiling and making gestures as he went.

He took her arm and they walked away from the crowds, finding a moment's shelter behind a row of mannequins impaled on meat hooks and lined up behind a sausage maker.

Martin took her arm and asked, "Well Armine, what's the take so far? Are we sold out? Can I leave yet?"

"You're not going anywhere, Martin. You're two hours late as it is, and I need your charm to move this stuff. Get out there and awe them with your grand artistic vision." Armine's thin lips curled, and her cobalt eyes shone cold beneath the shimmering curtain of her lacquered hair. "Put on that winning smile and go sweep those old women off their feet. Let's start selling."

"How have we done so far?"

"Oh, about thirty percent of the goods are reserved, mostly for all of your old sweethearts, and there's interest in the rest," Armine said. "The press seems receptive, so the reviews should draw people in. You need to schmooze the press, dear. Don't ever forget that."

She paused to look around the gallery. "The contraptions with moving parts are selling best. I'll have some dealers and curators from the Midwest here in a few days. We should be rid of it all by the end of next month," she said, cringing at the bloody meat hook above her. "I'll be glad to get rid of it. I feel like I'm working in Madame Tussaud's."

"No way, Armine, she did better work," said Martin, "but that gives me an idea: we could stick Prince Charles on a spit and have Princess Di roast him. His expression wouldn't change, would it? Always looks like he's fighting hemorrhoids anyway."

"Let's not offend the English, Martin. Some of those continental stuffed shirts are good customers, and I don't think they can take a joke directed at them or their precious royalty, not from this side of the Atlantic anyway."

She peered into the crowd from behind the torsos.

"Now look, Deborah Mondain's waiting for you. She's intrigued by that plastic slut on a stick over there, and she would like you to explain it to her."

"Why doesn't that surprise me?"

"Be nice to her and we've got a sale."

"Be nice? It's getting harder by the year to be nice to Deborah and her crowd."

She reached over, patted his cheek and said, "Now don't bite the hand that feeds you. Momma Deborah just wants a little attention from her talented young man, so go out there and sell her some, my little puppy-wupperkins."

Armine pouted her lips, smiled and then continued seriously, "We priced that piece at one-fifty, but I think that you can take her near two. Get her going, and I'll see if I can drum up somebody else to get a little bidding war going."

She led Martin back into the crowd, which parted around him. He gulped the last swallow of his whiskey and headed toward Deborah.

She was facing the other direction, toward the statue she admired. The wave of her blond hair rolled back and forth as she scanned the room, looking for the artist she so much wanted to talk to. Martin looked her up and down as he walked to her. She was well preserved for a woman of her age. Deborah's lines had long bent past the curves of girlhood, but she still possessed an expensive, pampered form molded from countless diets, years of tennis and the expertise of various personal trainers and pros. Martin knew she was still attractive to men twenty years her junior, but other signs were there: ankles beginning to bulge at the tops of her heels, thighs thicker than proportions allowed and a cushion of flesh padding her hips that simply couldn't be hidden or worked away.

As he moved toward her, his distaste grew. *When will I ever break out of this role of seducing and humping these vacuous old bags,* he asked himself. He sighed at the realization that he would only quit when he had enough of their money, of which he would never have enough. Or he would quit when they recognized him to be what he really was, a day he both dreaded and hoped for. *It's getting harder and harder to play the role, especially with this one,* Martin thought. He stopped a few feet behind Deborah so a waiter could freshen his drink. He took a swallow and then marched forward, deftly slinging an arm around her shoulders.

"Deborah, how good of you to come!" He looked into her wide, blue eyes—empty of all but adoration—and smiled, even as he recoiled within. He kissed her cheek and asked, "Well, what do you think of my exhibition?"

"Oh, I just love it, Martin! You're too horrid, too awful, too sexy. It's beautiful. Just beautiful. But, Martin," she said, as she laced her arm around his waist, "I'm not sure if I understand exactly what you're stating here?"

His coaxing smile veiled a mountain of contempt.

"What do you think I'm stating, dear?"

"Well, I don't know...I can see that she's in pain, but she doesn't seem hurt, not by her expression anyway. She looks as if she likes it. I don't know. I can't quite put my finger on it..."

Deborah contemplated the chemical blood dripping down to the plastic rats quivering at her feet.

"Martin, I just don't know. Can you help me? Just a hint, that's all."

As Martin casually studied the form, it almost seemed as if he had never seen it before, or if he had, that he didn't remember it. He looked down to read the brass plaque at its base. "Crucifixion of a Martyr" gleamed up from the brass.

He took his hand from around her shoulders and rubbed his chin in thought.

"Did you read the caption?" he asked.

"Yes, 'Crucifixion of a Martyr,' but she doesn't look like a martyr you would see in any church."

"Oh yes she does, Deborah. She's the martyr of this church, of this gallery…"

He smiled as his idea formed.

"Of this art. Can't you see it?" he asked.

Deborah's brows furrowed as her mind raced and became more confused. All of this thinking and all of the champagne she drank were making her hot. And the form above her massaging itself and the giant iron rod that pierced it, plus the incessant flow of blood running from the iron, made her feel a flow of her own. She wanted to leave the gallery that instant and take the artist with her, but she knew she couldn't have him now, not with the exhibition opening and not with Jonathan, her husband, at home entertaining his yacht club friends. *Why couldn't they hang around at the marina*, she wondered. And besides, she knew that in order to have Martin, she would have to buy something, and his work had become so gigantic and so expensive. Jonathan always complained about her new acquisitions and even laughed at them, but what did he know? He obviously just didn't understand art. He wouldn't understand this. She was sure of it.

She became more confused and asked, "Oh I'm sorry, Martin. Could you repeat what you just said? I'm a little giddy from all of this concentration."

"I said that she's the martyr of my art. She's the woman who gave me my start in this business and stood by me when I was little known and little appreciated. Look at how she accepts her martyrdom gladly. It's the justification for her confidence in my work, because everyone knows if the common man or critic can't understand something, well then it just might be good and valuable. Look!"

He became animated when he saw her forehead wrinkle while her mind scrambled to follow him. He chuckled to himself at her stupidity.

"Look at her hand massage her nipples! Look at her other hand lovingly massage the iron rod with which the masses impaled her. She's enraptured. She's orgasmic!"

He paused and waited for her to catch up, smiling down at her like a proud professor while thinking to himself, *let's see how much I can screw you for on this one, Deb.*

Deborah frowned. She was getting very excited about the sculpture's orgasm and was feeling a deep want of one herself, but the fact that he had created it in a woman's honor left her jealous. After all, she had supported him in his work for years, even in his lean years in The Village, where he would sometimes let her while away the hours watching him work and waiting expectantly for the occasional breaks he took to stop and hump her on his hard, cold studio floor and to teach her a little of art. Where was her statue after all her years of largess? Who was this bitch who got a statue? She felt angry blood rise to her cheeks. She withdrew her arm from around his waist and stared down at the rats in silence.

"Don't you want to know who this is, Deborah?"

She stared at the rats. She didn't want to know. She didn't want to be there. He was humiliating her again.

"It's you, Deborah. I sculpted this in honor of you. You are the mistress and the martyr of my work."

A wave swept over her face, transforming her jealous anger into joyous pride. She was a martyr of art! Deborah Mondain did have a purpose and nobody could take that from her. Jonathan and those women at the club scoffed at her taste and laughed at her purchases, but she had possessed an eye for art all along, an eye that none of them had. And now she was immortalized by the very sculptor that she helped to create, the world-famous Martin Drake. Oh, she wanted him inside her so badly. She'd have him soon—she knew it. After all, she was the martyr of his art. She wanted to feel his cold iron. She wanted the pain. She wanted to suffer. She was the martyr of his art!

She hugged him and choked back the tears. "Oh, Martin," she said, "it's the most beautiful thing I've ever seen in my life. You are a true genius! I must have it...and..." She looked around to see that no one was within hearing distance, then whispered, "Martin, I must have you. Let me give myself to you as you used to let me. Let me be your martyr again."

He kissed her on the cheek and whispered that he would stop by her townhouse the next day to help her position her new sculpture. Then he excused himself and walked away to tell Armine to bill her for the two. He knew she'd pay. She always paid.

Martin chuckled evilly to himself as he passed a Catholic priest who was gazing angrily around.

Chapter Two

THE DARK PRIEST MOVED through the gallery, glaring at the sculpture with an unveiled disgust that blew across his face like a gale across a cloudless sky, gusting darker with every step. His brown eyes smoldered with the anger that fishermen sometimes face, when after years of their greedy plundering, Mother Ocean rises to take her due. He stopped in front of the work entitled "Epiphany," which was a mannequin squatting atop a clear glass toilet, pants around its knees, staring up to the heavens with a look of rapture painted on its plastic face as it clutched a Bible to its chest and squeezed out a rubber tree boa. The snake wound its way round and round the bowl while munching a bright red apple that glistened yellow with the chemical urine that cascaded down upon it in a rivulet from above.

The priest studied the exhibit in hostile wonder, trying to fathom the diseased mind that could create such a thing. His broad shoulders tensed as he read the title of the work, and the muscles in his jaw flexed visibly like the gills of an angry shark. The veins in his hands stood out as he clenched them at his sides, hinting at the power within them. He stepped back and circled the work slowly, fury building as he pondered the mannequin and the rest of its kin spread across the room. *Why did Harry Banks ask me to meet him here*, he wondered. *What could this possibly have to do with my work? Where is God in this jumble of profanity and bad taste?*

As he circled and pondered, two ragged young people approached the mannequin and stood before it in obvious approval and admiration.

"This is just too cool," said the young man to his companion.

"Yeah," she replied. "Too cool!"

The priest smelled blood. He circled, looking for the man who had asked him to come here. He spotted Harry Banks, and, in a flash, he swam through the crowd toward him. Banks was talking with four others. Two were Banks' lawyers whom he had already met. One was a woman, beautiful in her evening dress, and the other was a tall man in black, somehow similar to himself. He dove into the group and accosted his possible benefactor in an agitated fury of accented English. "*Meu Deus*, Harry, what are we doing in this house of horrors? What kind of twisted person could be possessed to create such monstrosity?"

"That would be me, Father. I'm Martin Drake."

The priest turned to face Martin and drew himself back from the sculptor's outstretched hand. Rage swept his face, and his lips curled up as if he were ready to bite. He was handsome in his anger, a modern Moses confronting Aaron before the gilded calf. He glared at Martin, and Martin looked back, amused.

As they stood there, the two men seemed similar yet different, as if they were nearly duplicate portraits cast from the same spool of negatives. They were both tall and of a comparative build, but where the priest was solid, the sculptor was soft. Creases ran from the corners of their eyes and mouths, and their foreheads were crossed with deep parallel lines. The priest looked careworn and weathered, as though he had spent too many years under a burning sun in his quest for the salvation of man, while the sculptor wore the ravages of late nights, drugs and booze across his blanched face.

The real difference, though, was in their eyes. The priest's eyes burned in righteousness and flared into those of the artist, searching for an explanation for the malevolent expressions that surrounded them. His searching eyes were met for a moment by those of the artist, which flickered with cynical amusement and then flashed quickly to anger under the priest's continued gaze; it was the reactive, instinctive anger that comes to people when they meet a greater will. Martin's eyes broke away, looked to Armine and then to Harry Banks.

"And who is this," asked Martin, "the social reporter for the Christian Science Monitor?"

"Mr. Drake," said the industrialist, "this is Father Manoel da Silva Teixeira." He looked quickly to the priest to see if he had managed to pronounce the man's name correctly. The priest said nothing, so Banks continued, "Father Manoel is in the business of educating and feeding poor children in Brazil."

Martin looked confused, while Armine smiled blankly and responded, "Oh how interesting!" She proffered her hand, which the priest accepted.

"Father Manoel, this is Armine Quadras. She owns this gallery and is the exclusive agent for all of Mr. Drake's work. Mr. Drake has already introduced himself."

The priest glared once more at the artist, and then he, Martin and Armine turned back to Harry Banks, each hoping for an explanation.

"Well, you are all probably wondering what common interest you share."

The three nodded and Banks continued, concentrating on the artist who seemed uncomfortable in the presence of the priest, but who was more than willing to listen to anything the billionaire had to say.

"As I said, Father Manoel operates a charity in Brazil. He runs several daycare centers for the children of poor families. This allows both parents to work, thus providing a less miserable existence for the family. He feeds these children and shelters them during the day while their parents are working, and when they are old enough to enroll in public school, he provides them with the supplies and clothes they need to attend, and a hot lunch too. Without Father Manoel's help, these children would never have the chance of an education. He is struggling to break the cycle of poverty that has gripped his people from the outset of their history. I think this is noble. Don't you?"

Armine smiled at the priest and bobbed her head vigorously. Martin nodded to the billionaire and took another drink.

"That's wonderful of you, Father Manoel," said Armine with forced enthusiasm. "I would love to donate something to your cause."

The priest began to thank her, but Banks cut in.

"That's generous of you, Ms. Quadras, but I didn't bring Father Manoel here so I could solicit money for him."

Armine's labored smile turned to a look of confusion. All eyes were back on Banks. He pressed on. "No, I didn't come here to solicit donations. I came to make one.

"I have had a long and profitable association with Father Manoel's country. You are probably aware that I own one of the largest defense electronics and telecommunications corporations in the world. Well, I made my start in business in Brazil just before our entrance into World War II. In

15

those days there was a mad rush to produce the radios, radar and sonar we needed to beat the Germans and Japanese. But it wasn't like it is now. We couldn't produce all of the parts for our electronics domestically. Technology was basic. The transistor hadn't yet been invented. We relied on material that occurred naturally on Earth, and we were short, critically short, of two components vital to the war effort: quartz crystals for the production of radios and radars, and tourmaline crystals for the production of sonar. Without these crystals, our industry was paralyzed. We were at a great disadvantage.

"It was a crazy time. Men like me scoured the globe looking for the tons of crystals we so much needed to find. I spent months leading a pack mule, searching the mountains in Central Brazil with my miners and guides. The highlands were dangerous then, full of snakes and jaguars and desperate men. The law there was one of survival. But survive we did, and after a year of prospecting we found large deposits of the crystals we needed. I set up mining production and returned to the States to open my electronics factories.

After the war, our technology improved, and we learned to make synthetic crystals cheaper than we could mine them. My business grew in other areas, and I gradually forgot about my former holdings and my friends in South America."

Banks sighed and motioned for a waiter to bring him a glass of whiskey. Martin automatically freshened his glass. The waiter offered Father Manoel a glass, but he refused it. Armine was drinking Perrier.

The billionaire continued, "My wife, you must know of her, she ran our charity trust that gives heavily to the arts."

Martin and Armine said they did.

"Yes, I thought that you would have known her. Well, my dear Angeline passed away two months ago..."

Banks' small audience extended its condolences.

"Thank you," Banks said. "It has been hard, very hard. But one must survive, and I have her dear memory to keep me going.

"We were just married when I left for South America over fifty years ago. I've been reminiscing about those days a great deal lately, and consequently, I've started to remember my adventures in Brazil. As I've looked back over our lives, Angeline's and mine, I've come to realize that all of our good fortune was based on my mining strikes. We have given much to charity in this country, but I feel now that it's time to give something back to the people of Brazil. Without them and without their land, I would have been nothing. Who knows, without that quartz and tourmaline, we might have lost the war."

Banks turned to one of his lawyers, who was standing ready at his side, and asked, "George, may I have three of our pamphlets?"

The lawyer opened his briefcase and withdrew three color pamphlets, which he handed to his boss. Banks in turn passed them out to Martin, Armine and Father Manoel.

"These pamphlets describe the nature and range of the Banks Charitable Trust, of which I am now chairman after the death of my wife. We have given millions of dollars to charity over the last thirty years. We have been primarily involved in granting academic scholarships in the fields of engineering and the arts, but our grants have ventured into other areas as well. You are probably familiar with the Banks Children's Hospital?"

Armine said that she was. Martin, following her lead, said he was too.

"Yes. Well, that hospital has been a blessing to many children and is a favorite of mine, but the majority of our work over the past few years has been in the field of art. Angeline was a great believer in bringing art to the people, and as you can read in the brochure, we spend a great amount of money in acquiring art that we then auction off to museums at very low prices. Actually, I don't know why we just don't give it to the museums; you'd have to ask one of our accountants. Our methods are aimed at maximizing tax incentives, but at the moment, I can't recall the mechanics. Anyway, the money we receive from our auctions is used to fund various scholarships and the like, and this year I've decided to fund Father Manoel's daycare and educational program."

Father Manoel at once became pleased. "Why thank you very much, Harry. This is indeed great news!"

"It is nothing, Father," answered Banks. "This is a small thing. I love your country, and I would like to help in some meaningful way. From what I've heard, your work is very meaningful."

Father Manoel blushed at the compliment paid to him by one of the wealthiest men in the world and said, "Harry, you do me a great honor, but we only do what we must to give our children a chance at a better life."

"I believe that you do far more than that. Your reputation as a devoted crusader for the underclass precedes you. You bring hope to the hopeless and education to the ignorant. Hope is the motive force that spins this world, and it does spin, though slowly. Ignorance is the problem. It's the sand in the axle that grinds down our bearings to stall us. Keep that wheel spinning, Father," he said. "And let me give it a little grease now and then.

"What I would like you to do is to pick from this gallery several works of art that you feel are of merit, and I will buy them to donate to our trust for auction. The proceeds will then be yours to fund your work."

Father Manoel's expression changed from one of happiness and pride to one of exasperation, like a fisherman who just lost a prize marlin as he reeled it to the boat.

"*Ave Maria!* Harry, you can't ask me to do that. I can't begin to tell you how much we need money. Our funding expires in less than two months, and if I don't find a way I'm going to have to close down six of my centers—two thousand children will lose their place in school. But this..."

He looked around the room.

"I'm sorry, Harry, but I can't do it. I can't buy the future with blasphemy. It's sinful."

He looked to the ground. His brow furrowed in sorrowed frustration, and he clinched his hands together with such force that his fingers turned white at nail and knuckle.

He looked up slowly to Banks and said, "I thank you deeply, Harry, but I'm afraid I can't accept your generosity. I can't allow myself or the children I work for to be involved with such trash as I've seen tonight."

He patted the billionaire on the shoulder, then glared at Martin Drake as he began to walk away.

Martin glared back and took a swallow from his already empty glass. Armine stood with mouth agape, calculating the possible sale that was walking out the door.

Banks called out to the priest, "Father Manoel, please! Come back. I think that we can work this out."

The priest stopped, stood for a moment, hesitation showing in his shoulders. Then he turned and walked back to them.

"I agree with you, Father. What I've seen tonight hasn't set well with me either. You're right. This does not merit association with you or your church."

Martin started to say something, but Armine stopped him with a warning elbow to the ribs.

"Father," asked the billionaire. "What if Mr. Drake here were to sculpt something to your specification, something that you could appreciate?"

"Harry, I can't see this man sculpting anything that I could condone. I'm a priest not a pervert. I don't think I would be able to see the hand of God in anything he would create."

"Hand? Hell! Mr. Banks, I could cast a ten-foot face of God in bronze if the price was right," declared Martin, trying his best to remain calm and regain the sale.

Banks studied him for a moment and then turned to the priest. "Would you accept a bronze bust of the face of God, Father?"

"Honestly, Harry, I can't begin to tell you how badly we need money to carry on our work, but from what I've seen tonight, I don't think that I, in good conscience, could involve myself, my church or my children in any kind of sacrilegious display that this man might produce."

He glared again at the sculptor.

Banks looked at the priest, then the sculptor and his agent in turn.

"Would you agree to work with him if you had full artistic control of the project?"

The priest stared at the sculptor, whom he already disliked, then thought of the children in his charge. The weight of their dreams wore heavily on his shoulders. He couldn't say no. He swallowed ruefully and said a silent prayer. Softly, he answered, "Yes, I suppose if this man could find it in himself to create an image worthy of God...I suppose I could accept it."

Martin burst in. "Now wait a minute, I don't care how much money is involved, I won't have my art dictated by any Bible-thumping Amazonian!"

Armine jabbed him again, hard enough to take his breath. He heaved to get it back and looked at her in angered shock.

She took the billionaire's arm and said diplomatically, "Please Mr. Banks, come into my office. I'm sure that we can work this out."

"Yes, I think we can. Father Manoel, would you please wait out here? I'd like to have a word in private with Mr. Drake and Ms. Quadras."

He motioned for his lawyers to follow, and they all walked to Armine's office at the end of the gallery, leaving the priest alone amid Martin's art.

As they entered the office Banks turned to his lawyers and said, "Go ahead and get all the documents and have pens ready for signatures."

The lawyers sat down at Armine's wide table and opened their briefcases to pull out large sheaves of paper, which they began to sort.

Banks studied Martin and Armine, sizing them up. An industrialist who had achieved much in his lifetime, he was a good judge of people. Although he didn't relish dealing with these two, he was obligated in accordance with his late wife's wishes, so he would. They were greedy: they would be easy to deal with.

"Mr. Drake, Ms. Quadras, you have both heard me speak of my dear Angeline, and you are both aware of her contributions to the art world. My wife was conscientious in her acquisition of art, all art, to share with the people of this nation through donorship and subsidized sales to museum collections across the country. She was an old woman, but we came to our wealth early. As a result, she was a patron of most of the outstanding artists of this generation and the generation past.

As you are an artist," he nodded to Drake, "and you, the dealer of his art," he looked to Armine, "you may wonder why our charitable trust was so long in acquiring any of your work."

Armine clasped her hands to her breast and began to speak, but Banks waved her off and said, "Well, I'll tell you why she never bought any of your work. Quite frankly Angeline thought, and I think, your work a farce."

Martin and Armine both began to protest, but again he cut them off and continued.

"Angeline had scheduled purchases of your work years ago at the request of various museums, but I always vetoed the acquisitions. I recently began to assume the duties as chairman of our trust, my wife's former position, and I found that she again had succumbed to the wishes of certain curators and was planning to acquire a large amount of your sculpture. I find it harder to say no to her now that she's gone. No matter how distasteful I find this request, I will try to honor her position and will make the purchase.

"I do not appreciate your art, nor do I appreciate your public image, Mr. Drake. And from what I've seen tonight, I don't believe that I think much of you, either."

Martin feigned hurt. "Why Mr. Banks, I'm not used to being spoken to like this. My work and its acclaim speak for themselves. If you intend to treat me..."

"I will treat you as I see fit, young man."

The sculptor started to respond, but again Banks silenced him. "One million dollars."

Martin's jaw dropped, and Armine staggered and clutched the chair beside her.

"As a gesture to the memory of my wife, I will pay you one million dollars for a likeness of the face of God, but there is a catch. The design and final work must be approved by Father Manoel. Will you agree to this?"

Martin started to air an objection, but before he could, Armine said, "Why, Mr. Banks, as Mr. Drake's agent and exclusive dealer I can assure you that he would be able to fulfill your contract without reservation."

"Drake?" queried Banks.

Armine stuck a thumb in Martin's kidney.

Martin swallowed and slowly answered. "No, Mr. Banks, no reservations at all."

"Good, good. I'm glad we all understand each other. Now if I may be so bold, Ms. Quadras, I need the use of your office. Could you two please leave us and send in Father Manoel. Thank you."

Banks turned toward his lawyers, ending the discussion. He spoke to them about various contractual issues and waited to hear the door shut behind him.

Chapter Three

MARTIN AWOKE WITH A start to the ringing of his telephone. Although it roused him, it wasn't as loud as the drum that sounded in his head. He rolled to answer the phone, then rolled the other way when he heard the rustle of sheets behind him. There was a young girl in bed with him, not over twenty, he guessed. Pretty, but nothing special. He smiled at her benignly, then reached for the phone.

"Hello," he mumbled into the receiver.

"Why hello and good afternoon, sweet pea!"

"Look, Armine, I'm a little busy here..."

"That's splendid, Martin. I didn't think you ever got busy before the sun went down. Now get out of bed and talk to me. You have a full day ahead of you."

"I'll call you in a little while." He hung up.

Martin turned and looked into the eyes of the girl, who was staring at him in obvious adoration. *Who was she*, he wondered. He tried to remember the previous night. There had been the ordeal with Banks and that bastard of a priest that Banks drug along. He cringed. His head throbbed as he pictured the faces of the tough old industrialist and the glaring, angry priest. They saw right through him, and that galled him. Then he remembered the contract they'd signed for the million-dollar sculpture of the face of God to be delivered in two months. The painful thrumming in his head softened at the thought of all that money. He smiled, and the girl smiled back. Her big eyes grew even bigger.

Oh yes, he had been trying to place her. Instead, his mind kept coming back to the feeling that he'd been somehow coerced into signing that contract. No one forced him into anything, yet he felt uneasy when he signed it. It was as if his love of money had betrayed him; it had delivered him into the hands of that zealous Brazilian. The drumming in his head came back to life. Then he remembered the girl. After Banks and the priest left, he had stalked back into the gallery seeing red. A million bucks or not, he was angry. Banks had belittled him, and the priest had unnerved him with the silent accusations flaring from his eyes. He wanted revenge. The girl was there with her boyfriend, art students by the look of them. He led her away and had her in his car within minutes. Now he knew. She was nobody, nobody that he had to be nice to anyway. He stopped smiling. He wanted her out of the house.

"Well, thanks for stopping over," he said bluntly. "You can show yourself out."

He left the girl in his bed just as shock and hurt began to show on her young, pretty face. Then he stumbled to his bathroom, opened the medicine cabinet and reached for his Advil. He shook out two pills then another. After gulping them dry, he headed out the door. As he was leaving, he happened to glance at his reflection in the mirror: he didn't like what he saw. He moved quickly away and down the hall to his large kitchen.

Martin started a pot of coffee and pulled a cup from the cupboard above the sink. Water ran over the rim and splashed into the sink as he filled it. He drank several cups, downing them as fast as he could. Then he shuffled over to the kitchen counter and sat down, cradling his pounding head in his hands.

When the drip coffee maker gurgled its announcement of fresh coffee, Martin took the carafe off the hot plate and returned to the counter, where he poured himself a cup. When the cup was half-full, he stopped pouring. He set the carafe down and topped off the cup with whiskey from a bottle on the countertop. This he drank, then made himself another. He was just starting on it when the phone rang. He picked it up and was accosted with, "I thought you were going to call me back, Martin. Today's a busy day. You've got work to do."

"I was just about to call, Armine. I had a little business of my own to take care of."

"Well, if you're not done by now, I'm sure that she will keep until tomorrow, whoever she is. Zip up and wake up. Did you read Peter Bailey's review in *The Times*?"

"No Armine, I didn't get to the paper yet..."

"No, I suppose not. It's only one-thirty in the afternoon. I can't imagine anyone reading the paper before six. I only do it to save you the trouble. I wouldn't want your delicate, aesthetic sensibility shocked by anything newsworthy."

"Marry me, Armine," he breathed into the phone.

"Sorry, Martin. A roll with you now and then might not be bad, but to tell you the truth, the way you live your life...I'm afraid I might end up catching something I couldn't get rid of. You know us girls diet like crazy to stay slim, but I don't want to lose weight like that. No, sweet cheeks, as much as I'd like to marry you, I'm afraid I'm destined to dream of you."

"Fuck you, Armine."

"Now, Martin, we just went over that. Forget the romance. Don't you want to know how much money you made yesterday?"

He sat up straight at the mention of money.

"Yes, darling," he whispered. "Talk dirty to me."

"Do I ever do anything else? But first the reviews: your adorable little troll devoted a column to the 'renewed proof of genius exhibited by sculptor Martin Drake, a man destined to be remembered as one of the premier artists of the latter half of this century.' Now there's a candidate for marriage."

"Latter half of the century, huh? That's only fifty years. Why couldn't he have written century or age or something? And I thought Peter cared. No, Armine, he'll never win me with such paltry praise as that."

"You received the normal accolades in *The Post* too."

"Good. Now what about money?"

"Martin we grossed $1.4 million if you include the contract with Harry Banks. He's a mean old bastard, isn't he? But his money's sweet. A million dollars, Martin, for a single bust! Can you believe it? That's the biggest sale you've ever had."

A sinking feeling grew in Martin's belly. The drums began to sound.

"I'll have to earn it, Armine. God, can you imagine working with that Latino holy avenger breathing down your neck. Look, I want you to keep that priest away from me as much as you can. He makes me nervous. You can't expect me to get anything done with him looking on."

"Not the kind of stuff you get done, sweet cheeks, but I'll see what I can do. He called this morning all in a rush to get started. Apparently, he needs the money from the auction of your piece as soon as possible. Our contract has a two-month deadline, but he seems intent on moving as quickly as he can. I told him to meet me in my office tomorrow morning. I'll show him the catalogues of all your previous work to see if we can find something to sell him that he'll take without too much protest. His time restrictions could work in our favor. It's funny, I think that he actually expects to see you in the gallery with a chisel in hand, ready to lay into a block of marble.

"I'll do what I can to keep you two at a distance, but you're going to have to deal with him eventually—after all, you're the genius he hired. From your reaction yesterday, I gather that he gives you indigestion. Haven't been to confession in a while have you, sweet cheeks?"

Martin grumbled and sipped his coffee but said nothing.

Armine continued, "Well skip the confession until tomorrow, Martin. Remember that you have an appointment this afternoon with Deborah Mondain. If you confess now, you won't get much mileage out of it."

He cringed at the reminder of his appointment. "When am I supposed to see her?" he asked.

"She called this morning and said that she would be free at four. I told her you'd be there."

"Thanks, Armine. Thanks a lot. I can always count on you. Anything else?"

"Not for today, dear. I just called to make sure you got over to see Momma Deborah on time. We have a meeting tomorrow at four p.m. at the gallery to discuss new designs. Oh, there is one other thing—Vicki's bitching about the new artists you hired. She says they're giving her a hard time."

Martin downed his coffee and refilled his cup with straight whiskey. "If I hire men, she says they give her a hard time. If I hire women, she can't keep her paws off them and chases them out of the studio within weeks. I'm starting to worry about sexual harassment suits. If we are involved in a lawsuit, it had better damn well be me who does the harassing. I don't want to pay for her pleasure. If she weren't such a vicious, perverted dyke, I'd have fired her years ago, but nobody can come up with ideas like Vicki does. And nobody but Vicki would let me exploit them so badly.

"I'll have a talk with those new guys tomorrow. We have to treat our rabid little Vicki as the princess that she is."

"Talk to them today, Martin. Vicki's insistent. She called twice this morning." Armine laughed. "Well, that's all I have for you. Don't forget about our meeting tomorrow and give my best to Deborah. Tell her that we'll deliver in two weeks; the piece has to remain on display with the rest of exhibition until then. Have fun, lover!"

Martin growled into his receiver and then flung it toward its base, where it clattered home. He looked at his watch and saw that it was nearly two. He needed to get moving. As he walked to the shower he wondered where he would lunch.

Chapter Four

"THANK YOU, PHILIP," SAID Martin as the concierge sat him at his favorite table.

He was used to eating well. As a matter of business, he often lunched with his patrons at the finest restaurants in the city. He knew them all and frequented them in a cycle of regularity and repetition: Lutece, Parioli Romanissimo, The Four Seasons, The Quilted Giraffe. Round and round he went, smiling and laughing for people he could no longer stand, and indulging in gourmet delights that bored him. Good food had lost its appeal, as had most conversation and most women. He had been gluttonous in all his desires for so long that nothing held any taste.

Armine would generally set his lunch and dinner schedule. He had to do nothing more than show up, espouse his theories on art and try to remain fairly sober and somewhat charming. Ten years ago, he loved the exposure and the chance to meet the people of power who ran the city and country. He had loved to tread in the ways of the rich and famous. He had flushed when they were interested in his work. But that flush had fled with his youth. Now he only felt tedium, and the stirrings of loathing and contempt.

This was his restaurant, though. It was just a block from his apartment, and it was not on the circuit. Although it served outstanding food and had the air of a truly great restaurant, it was relatively unknown, a diamond in the rough yet to be gouged from obscurity and thrust up to glimmer amid the glitter of his empty world. It was small and safe. It was *his* place.

A waiter quickly marched up with the wine list. Martin scanned it and then declined to select a wine, asking instead for a double Glenlivet. He knew that whiskey deadened the palate and buried the delicate flavors of fine food, but he had long since lost his taste. He preferred the tongue-numbing effect of the whiskey. The waiter left with Martin's drink order, and the *maître d'* walked up to his table to greet him.

"Good afternoon, Mr. Drake, I hope the day finds you well."

"Hi Andre. What's cookin'?" He smiled up at the fat Frenchman, who beamed back at his valued customer.

"Today, Mr. Drake, we have *Bifteck à la provençale*: a luscious tenderloin of beef simmered in olive oil with mushrooms, garlic and eggs, served with asparagus and baked potato. We have *Escalopes panées au gruyère*: breaded veal scallops simmered in butter, stuffed with *gruyère* cheese, served with lemon and creamed spinach. We have *Canard à la rouennaise*: roasted duck bathed in a wonderful sauce of butter, wine, cognac and pâté de foie du canard. This is served with wild rice and creamed lettuce."

Martin held up a hand to kill the recitation, which he knew would drone on for another two minutes, leaving him totally lost and destined to have it repeated again.

"Enough, Andre. Do you have any fish?"

"Yes of course, Mr. Drake. We have *Truite au bleu*: fine trout marinated in red wine and quick boiled in vinegar, served with butter in a parsley garnish on a bed of boiled potatoes. We have..."

31

"That sounds good. I'll try the trout."

"A fine choice, sir. I'm sure you will enjoy."

Andre bowed slightly and motioned to one of the waiters nearby. He placed Martin's order while moving on to another table where other guests had just been seated.

Martin's drink arrived, and he sipped it slowly. Already, early in the day, he could barely sense the smoke in the single malt that puffed around his tongue. *An afternoon with Deborah, what a treat*, he thought. He took another swallow and stared down at the tablecloth, wondering when his headache would pass. It would probably stick with him until that evening, until after he put in time with Deborah.

Two waiters approached, one with a salad plate and another with a breadbasket and pâtés. He reached for a hard roll, broke it in half and covered it with butter. He chewed it and thought of the moment to come. He would show up and be ushered into the foyer by Deborah's butler, who would shuffle off to fetch her. Then after several minutes, she would appear at the balcony and slowly descend the stairs wearing something that would show the turn of her legs—a turn for the worse, he mused. The years had been kind to her, but not that kind.

Ten years ago, he delighted in wowing her with art theory and then womping her, first with his prick and then with his prices. She was beautiful then, dumb but beautiful. Beautiful and rich! She was still dumb and still rich, but no longer beautiful. Ten years was a long time.

What would the next ten years bring? In a flash he saw himself atop a sixty-year-old Deborah. He cringed and traded the half-eaten roll for his glass, from which he took a large swallow. The Banks job might give him the freedom to walk away from some of his older, more revolting clients. His relationship with Deborah was unique, really. Most of the others were just interested in brushing against his genius in the hope that it might color their expensive, but gray and wasted, lives.

By entering their circle and creating the illusion that they were the privileged few who understood and supported what he did, he gave them what they wanted—although he knew he was cheating them. That, however, didn't bother him a bit. He enjoyed it. Lately, though, it had become a bore, and now he wished that he could steal from them outright. Maybe this deal with Banks would allow him to snub his more boorish patrons and move up to an even more exclusive clientele. Sales breed sales, and price breeds price. He would have to talk to Armine about raising theirs. Maybe Deborah wouldn't be able to afford him in the future. *Oh yes she would*, he realized. Her parents had created a moron as stupid as their fortune was vast. She would always be rich enough and dumb enough to pay. And if she could pay, he knew that he would always play.

Greed wasn't a vice to him; it was the rock on which his house was founded. It was all he had left, and he clung to it desperately. *Greed's my creed*, he chuckled to himself. Greed's my god, and I do everything to worship him and give him thanks...and to wheedle him for more. He wondered if the priest would go for a big bronze dollar sign. His joke turned sour at the thought of the priest.

The trout arrived in a sea of potatoes and butter. It stared up at him with its glazed, dead eye as he looked down at it dully. He picked up a piece with his fork, placed it in his mouth and began to chew while he thought about Deborah and the girl he had found in his bed. Why couldn't he meet an interesting woman? They're all Deborahs in one way or another, but then he rarely gave anyone a chance. He couldn't remember the last time he was totally captivated by a woman. Oh he could remember; he could remember well, but he chose not to. It hurt to remember, and Martin didn't like to hurt, though he really never stopped feeling the dull ache of loss for the one he couldn't forget.

The only woman that even slightly interested him anymore was Armine. Perhaps Vicki, but only as an object of scientific wonder, certainly not of romance. Just the thought of it made him queasy, and besides, Vicki didn't swing his way. She had been working for him for years, and in all that time he could never quite believe her zealous determination in the construction of their abominations. She was so dedicated to their work and so sincere about her art, art which he found laughable, a great joke on a world populated by dunces. She was a crusader of the faith, a standard bearer of perversion. She was totally mad.

Armine, though, was not. She was a cat, a vampire cat, lithe, smooth, silky and deadly. Blood ran cold in her veins. Never had he met an operator like her, so charming, so sweet, so beguiling and so very, very unprincipled. She'd sell children for kindling if she could profit by it. Armine was truly an interesting woman. The only thing she lacked was a heart. There was an attraction between them. There always had been, but they both laughed it off, knowing each other as they did. No, for him women were just another hunger he could never quite sate. His plate seemed always full, but was actually always empty.

Martin reached down to finish the trout. It was just bones now, bones and head, a shipwreck strung along potatoed sands. He picked at its ribs and realized he couldn't remember what it tasted like. Its dead eye stared up at him in blind accusation. He stared back for a moment and thought he saw the rage of the priest, the contempt of the billionaire and the hurt of the young girl in his bed, all flickering below its cloudy membrane. He blinked and looked again. It was lifeless and empty. Then he remembered his own eyes in the bathroom mirror that morning. He shuddered and gouged the eye with his fork. He looked up and motioned for another Scotch and the check.

The check arrived quickly, just after the Scotch he had already downed. He handed a credit card to his waiter, who whisked it off to the register. Gloom filled him as he stared unfocused into the whiteness of the tablecloth spread before him. He never felt good, but he usually didn't feel this bad. The numbness he carefully cultivated fled when faced with the dull pounding depression that beat from deep within him. He longed for days far gone when he cared about his work and about somebody else. Memories of a woman whispered faintly from the past. Why couldn't he meet somebody like her again? Why couldn't he have another chance? Maybe that would make all the difference...

"Why Martin Drake, you've the look of a man possessed. Conjuring up another sculpture?"

Startled, he looked up. It was Emily Buckman, matriarch of the New York Buckmans, barons of paper and publishing.

"Hello Emily," he said, as he rose to greet her. "I didn't think that anyone knew about my little hideaway."

"It won't be your hideaway for long, darling. Belle Shanks raves about the place. She says the food is marvelous, so I brought my niece here to try it. Martin Drake, I'd like you to meet Amanda Stalwart. Amanda, this is Martin."

Martin reached out and took the hand of the stunning woman before him. She was perhaps five years his junior, dressed severely in a business suit with her hair pulled back. Try as she might, she could do nothing to dull the edge of her beauty. She looked at him directly with cool blue eyes that glinted with purposeful intelligence.

35

"This is quite a treat, Amanda," said Emily. "One doesn't often bump into an artist of Martin's reputation."

"Are you an artist, Mr. Drake?"

"I've been called worse, Amanda, but in this case and in probably most others, the name fits. Yes, I am an artist, a sculptor really."

"That's wonderful. I love art. As a matter of fact we are shopping for sculpture for a building we are putting up in Cincinnati."

"Amanda is vice president of Buckman Publishing's Central Division," interjected Emily with a smile. "She's one of our youngest vice presidents and is certainly the best."

"I don't know about that, Aunt Emily, but thanks."

"Why don't you show Amanda some of your work, Martin? I don't know how well acquainted she is with the New York art scene. She may not be familiar with what you young men are doing here. I don't think the reverberations of your shockwave have quite reached Cincinnati. They still admire Michelangelo and Rodin."

"One can't help but admire the masters, Emily. Everything is relevant when viewed in context with its time. I would be delighted to show Amanda my work. I just opened a new exhibition at the Quadras gallery last night, and I'd be happy to walk you both through it."

"Martin, I'm getting too old to look at your work. As you said, everything—and everyone—is relevant to the context of their time, and darling, I'll have to admit you're a little beyond mine. Why, I was even unsure about Andy Warhol for heaven's sake!" She pressed a hand to her cheek and laughed. "No, Martin, I'll stick with Michelangelo. Amanda, however, might enjoy you. She's today. I was the week before last."

Martin feigned disbelief. "If you are the week before last, then I'm nostalgic. In any event, I am at the service of you both."

They smiled.

"Martin, could you do me the biggest of favors?" asked Emily. "Roland and I have an engagement tonight that we simply can't break. Do you suppose that you could take charge of Amanda and show her your work this evening?"

Amanda looked to Martin and said, "I'm afraid I'm a little bit difficult for anyone to take charge of, but I would enjoy seeing your work. Aunt Emily has me intrigued."

"Amanda, it would be a pleasure. Nine o'clock sound good?"

"That would be wonderful."

"Great, where are you staying? I'll pick you up."

"I'm at Aunt Emily's. Which is..."

"I know it. It's a landmark. So, I'll pick you up at nine then." He looked at his watch, which read 4:15. "God, I'm late. I have to run. Emily, it's always a pleasure. Amanda, it's nice to have met you."

"And it was nice to meet you, Mr. Drake."

Martin picked up his credit card and placed it in his wallet.

"Take good care of my niece, young man," said Emily.

"You may rest easy tonight, Emily," said Martin, giving them a wave as he walked out the door.

"Did you smell his breath, Aunt Emily?" asked Amanda as they followed Philip to their table. "Stone drunk at four in the afternoon. The life of an artist must be difficult."

Chapter Five

MARTIN PAID OFF HIS taxi, then climbed the steps of the grand townhouse on the Upper West Side. He rang the bell and was momentarily ushered in by Deborah's butler.

"Ah, good afternoon, Mr. Drake," said the ancient servant. "Mrs. Mondain has been expecting you. Please wait a moment while I inform her of your arrival."

"Thanks, Herbert."

Herbert moved away, then hesitated for a moment as if trying to remember something he had forgotten to do. He turned and walked back to Martin.

"Forgive me, sir. Your coat, may I take it for you?"

Martin took off his coat and handed it to the butler who moved to the august staircase that swept to the balcony above. Again, he stopped, looking to the coat on his arm and then to the stairs before him. He seemed to be battling with a decision. Finally, he shrugged and began to creak upward. Martin watched his careful ascent as he ever so slowly disappeared from view.

He definitely belongs here, thought Martin. *Those two could talk brain surgery.* He paced back and forth, studying the baroque design in the marble floor. Fat, rosy cherubs smiled up at him and spread garlands at his feet. *Must have been Deborah's grandma who chose this*, he thought. He scowled at the cherubs and scuffed one's face with the heel of his shoe.

Martin thought about the woman he had met at lunch, Amanda, the publisher. Now *she* was a woman. He tingled at the thought of her and wondered what she did as a publisher, the decisions she made, the power she had over the people who worked for her. I bet she enjoys her work, he mused. She's probably the kind that leaves the office late and goes in early. He sensed a passion in her, a real passion, and a power of will. He hadn't felt passion in so long that he rarely even thought about it. Vicki had passion, but hers was just the bent energy of someone long past over the edge. Armine had passion too, but then it wasn't really passion was it? It was more like hunger, what a diamondback feels for a desert rat. No, Amanda had something they didn't have. He divined a sense of purpose in Amanda, the kind that came from liking what you're doing and being good at it. He wanted to get to know her. He wanted to talk to her and, of course, he wanted to touch her. Martin knew that she would be a conquest that he wouldn't soon forget.

"Ah, Martin, I see you finally made it," said Deborah from the balcony. "I was afraid you had forgotten our appointment."

"Forget an appointment with you, Deborah? Why, I could never do that." He caught the irony in his statement even as he spoke it. "No, Deborah, I didn't forget our meeting. I was hung up with another patron. Someone who's interested in commissioning sculpture for a new building. Sorry, I just couldn't get away."

"You're forgiven, Martin," she said, beginning to slowly descend the stairs. She was wearing a tight silk blouse and a skirt that reached mid-thigh. It was an appropriate outfit, not overtly sensual, yet cut a little too boldly for a woman of her age and build to be wearing at home in the afternoon. As she slinked down to meet him, he smiled into her hungry eyes and wished he had a drink.

She walked across the foyer, embraced him and whispered in his ear. "Oh, Martin, I've missed you so. It's been so long since we've had a moment together. It's hard to be a martyr, Martin. One suffers terribly."

He brushed her ear with his lips and whispered back. "The life of the blessed was meant to be so, but isn't the reward worth the price? Think of what you've given the world, Deborah. It was you who inspired me."

She pulled away as she heard the shuffling steps of Herbert. Looking up, she saw him at the head of the stairs, Martin's coat still slung across his arm, preparing for his downward climb.

"Herbert, that will be all for now, thank you," she said. "I will be showing Mr. Drake the house."

He stopped, both feet on a stair, and answered, "Very well, Madame."

He renewed his descent.

"So, Deborah, where are we going to put your statue. What room in this house might best compliment it?"

"I'm not sure, Martin. You know our house. What do you think?"

He smiled. "Why not place my martyr here, surrounded by all of these little angels?" He took the chance to scuff another cherub with the tip of a pointing foot.

"I don't know if Jonathan would approve of your sculpture in the foyer, Martin. You know how conservative he is. So smart in business but so lost in art. He keeps buying those silly Remington bronzes for God's sake. There are little cowboys galloping around the entire house. Honestly, he's such a Neanderthal about some things."

Martin squeezed her arm and gave her a pitied shrug.

"It's sad to say, Deborah, but not everyone has your good taste. It's hard to be a swan in a puddle of ducks isn't it, Darling? All of their incessant quacking and constant preening are enough to drive one mad."

Just like you do to me, he thought. "Why don't we walk around and see where we can best place your tribute."

He led her into one of the adjacent rooms and asked as they went, "Deborah, would you mind if I have a glass of Scotch while we look around, I've had a difficult day. I'll pour. I don't want Herbert to trouble himself. And anyway, he's still working on hanging my coat."

"Of course, I don't mind," she answered, though mind she did because he was already thick with the smell of booze, and more might affect the afternoon she had planned for them.

"Thanks, sweet." He patted her behind as they walked to the bar across her large dining room. He poured three fingers, swallowed one right off, breathed deeply and asked, "Where shall we begin?"

She looked at her watch. They were late, and she didn't want to spend much time on this.

"Why don't we start here, dear. I'll just walk you through, and you see what you think."

She put her arm around his waist and led him away from the bar. As they walked from room to room, Martin made a show of checking the lighting, natural and electric, while wondering quietly to himself where he might place the statue to give it the maximum amount of exposure to her guests while not raising too many objections from her husband. He walked slowly and took his time, explaining to her the intricacies of lighting and the importance of environment: a room and its furnishings could greatly detract from a work's impact if they were not complementary to it. He might have to model a room exclusively for the sculpture to do it justice.

Deborah wasn't listening. She'd been waiting all morning, and now Martin was moving too slow. They had spent forty minutes looking for a place and had not yet covered the first floor of the north wing. He was almost done with his drink, and he'd surely ask for another. Artists were so self-destructive, weren't they? She had to have him before he self-destructed, that day anyway. Jonathan would be home in less than two hours. "Martin, dear, I think I have just the place for my statue."

"We don't want it too close to any of my earlier works, Deborah, they aren't complementary. Different styles and themes..."

"No. No. Wait and see. There's nothing else of yours there. Come and see."

She took his hand and led him back to the foyer to the grand stairs from which she had earlier descended. He saw the stairway and knew that it was time. With a final swig, he reluctantly followed her up.

"Well, here we are," she said, as she closed the door behind her and locked it.

"You want your martyr in your bedroom, sweet?" he asked as he backed away.

"No, I want my artist! I want you to have your martyr. Take me!"

She flew into his arms and began to kiss him wildly. Her tongue probed deep down his gaping mouth. She kissed him hungrily as he gasped for air. She unbuttoned his shirt and kissed the mat of hair beneath it as she pulled at his belt and zipper.

He absently patted her head with one hand as he moved his other to bring up his glass. Seeing it empty, he dropped it to the floor.

Pants slid free, and she tugged at his underwear to get at his still flaccid organ. She pulled it out and began to kiss and stroke it violently. Martin stared down dumbly at the top of the head he knew so well as Deborah pumped him with her mouth and yanked off her blouse. Then she kicked off her shoes and wriggled out of her skirt, still working madly to bring his manhood to life. He looked down at her, now in lacy bra and tiny panties, and stroked her hair as he watched the way her flesh bunched out to almost roll over the slim line of fabric that covered her sex. Her bra strap dug a trench in the softness of her back. Repulsed, he moved to take a step backward, but his pants tripped him up, causing him to fall with the inert thud of a true dead drunk.

She was atop him at once, pulling at him with one hand and cradling his head with the other. She dove deep inside his mouth, her tongue on his, twining it in reptilian passion. She pulled her panties off and rubbed herself into him with heated, lustful grunts, but it was all for nothing: he lay beneath her inert and glassy eyed.

Deborah looked down at him a moment and said with compassion, "We had a little too much to drink this afternoon, didn't we, my artist?"

"Yeah, I guess so, Deborah. I guess I did."

"That's all right, Martin. Your martyr's going to fix you up."

She climbed off him and then pulled off his shoes, socks and pants, which were in a tangle about his hairy ankles. She helped him up, led him to her bed and then walked over to a closet. While she did so, he stared dully at all that her clothes could hide: the beginnings of love handles starting to break above her widening hips, her fleshy back, her dimpled ass. He honestly knew that for her age she was uncommonly attractive and that she had kept herself in much better condition than he had, but even in his drunkenness he despised her and loathed her touch.

Shoes flew from the closet as she rummaged through it. Momentarily she came out with a little bag of white powder. She picked up a mirror off her dressing table and returned to the bed, where she sat down beside him and carefully arranged two lines of coke.

"Have a little toot, darling; it will sober you up."

Martin bent down to the mirror and drew in both lines with practiced snorts. At once, the clouds began to clear in his head. The fog rolled back above the fire and in minutes he was ready to go. He felt the power he knew as a youngster while working with clay. Blood rushed loudly through his veins, but when he glanced down between his legs to see Deborah fiercely stroking him, he knew it wouldn't be enough. Anger flushed his cheeks. Why, if this stupid cow wanted him so badly, couldn't she be more attractive or more interesting? Why couldn't she accept his excuses and leave him alone? Why did she have to slobber so damn much? He reached down and grabbed her hair in a clenched fist. She moaned and worked him harder. He was angry at his impotence and blamed her for its cause. *Who the fuck would want to screw you anyway?* But he wasn't going fail; cow or not, he'd fuck her. *Why can't you be like Amanda*, he thought. *Yes! Amanda!* Amanda, how beautiful she was in her business suit, and how much more beautiful she must be without it. An image of her naked in his arms danced in his mind, and he felt faint stirrings down below.

"Yes! Oh yes," slurred Deborah from around the mass of his hardening member.

He glared down at her, then returned to his dream. He'd see Amanda tonight, and he might have a chance with her if she liked his work and if she found him charming. She would. *He knew it.* He was Martin Drake, renowned sculptor. He was famous. He felt the power in his veins. He was a rock!

Martin reached down to roughly flip Deborah over. She quivered in anticipation and quickly got up on her hands and knees. She felt his fingers searching her and gasped at the feel of his hard heat between her legs. Then she tensed.

"No, Martin, not like that. You know I don't like it that way."

He slapped her hard on her buttocks. "Are you my martyr, Deborah?"

"Oh yes, Martin! Yes, but not that way. It hurts me that way...ooh!" she cried out and grasped the carpet as he pushed deep inside her.

"Suffer for me, Deborah. Suffer for your sculptor, my martyr."

"Oh. Oh yes, Martin. Oh yes!" Her pain slowly turned to pleasure as he lost himself in dreams of Amanda.

Chapter Six

"HELLO, MR. DRAKE, I hope I didn't keep you waiting long. I just received a phone call that I had to take," said Amanda, as she walked across the sitting room with her gloves in one hand and her coat neatly across her arm.

"Nothing serious, I hope." Martin stood to meet her and took her hand.

"No, nothing that important." She slid into her thick wool coat and began to button it. "I'm having trouble with an author of ours who wants to make major changes in a book we have ready to print. I'm afraid he called me too late: I can't afford to stop the presses now. We have too much invested. He's in a rage and is threatening to sue. Such foul language from a man who writes so beautifully, I was a little shocked. I've known him for years, a very intense man, obsessed really. I'd like to accommodate him, but I just can't."

Amanda looked down as she pulled on her tight leather gloves and said, "He delivered the book, approved the edited proofs and seemed happy with them when he last spoke to his editor. Not a word until tonight, the night before the first press run, and now he's screaming to have it stopped."

"I hope he didn't upset you."

"No, Mr. Drake..."

"Call me Martin."

"All right, Martin, then. No, he didn't upset me. I've dealt with this enough not to be affected by it. Almost every established novelist I know is a *prima donna*. I'll stand my ground, and he'll have no choice but to accept the printing—he signed the contract after all. When he reads the first good reviews, he'll calm down, and all will be forgotten."

"It sounds as if your job is tough," he said, as they moved to the door.

"No, I think my job is relatively easy compared to that of the writers whom I work with. I deal with the occasional demon that escapes them from time to time, but they continually wrestle with the rest. I have great respect for our better novelists. Their work does not come easy. Some of them agonize dreadfully over things that seem trivial to me. I imagine your work as a sculptor must be of a similar nature."

They walked down the grand entrance of the Buckman mansion to Martin's Porsche parked below.

"We all have our demons; it's true. You shall meet some of mine tonight at the gallery."

She caught a waft of his breath and knew that she already had.

Martin disarmed his car alarm with a beep and a flash of headlights, then opened the passenger door. He expected her to enter, but she stopped a moment to study his face. "Are you sure you're okay to drive?"

"Of course, I'm okay. Why do you ask?"

"I don't mean to be rude, but I noticed that you seem to have had a bit to drink."

Martin flushed. He hadn't had a D.U.I in over two years. He knew what he was doing. This Amanda could be bitchy, couldn't she? Well, she'd give him a little leeway when she saw his work. Artists were allowed their quirks after all.

"Oh, I had a whiskey an hour ago, but I'm fine to drive."

She looked him over, then reluctantly got into the car and pulled in her door, which sounded with the concise thunk of fine German engineering. Martin walked around, entered the car and fired the engine. It entered a broody wakefulness and then growled to life as he gunned it into the street. Martin wove through traffic, cutting it close to the cars he passed and jerking to stops at the traffic lights he couldn't beat. He could feel the revs of the engine as it pulsed its power toward the pavement below. He felt it was part of him. The powder he took from Deborah was still with him, making him feel like a god. As he drove, he talked about art.

"Are you much interested in art, Amanda?" he asked, as he heeled into a screeching right turn.

She waited for the car to settle itself before responding. "I enjoy art. I studied art history in college, of course, and I used to go to museums quite often when I had the time, when I was a student mostly. My job doesn't allow me much time for the finer things in life, I'm afraid. My husband was always nagging me to spend time with him at various exhibitions in galleries and museums, and at the occasional house of a friend, but I just never had the time."

"Are you married?"

"No, divorced."

"I'm sorry to hear that," said Martin, who clearly wasn't.

"Don't be. It was my choice. I found that I simply couldn't give him everything he asked for, and he was always asking for something: my time, my attention, my constant support and encouragement in whatever little whim that moved him at the moment. He couldn't concentrate on anything for very long, and the only thing that seemed critical for him was my approval. I couldn't approve anymore. I outgrew him."

She leveled her eyes at Martin for a moment and then stared back out the windshield.

Martin turned and gazed at her. She was a woman all right. He looked her over, starting at her thin ankles then moving slowly up her body, which was still encased in the warmth of her coat. His eyes rested on her face and studied her silhouette, accented by the mass of her hair and by the momentary flash of passing street lamps. Her fine features were heightened by the shadows that they cast and by the disciplined tautness in which she held them. She was beautiful in her sober fierceness, and she was acute, acute enough surely to appreciate the man of talent beside her. His nose tingled and his heart pulsed with powdered energy. She would not be able to resist a man of talent and passion such as he. He pictured taking her on the gallery floor, surrounded by the fruit of his creation. He felt a throbbing down below.

"Watch out!"

He screeched to a stop, mid-intersection, just missing a passing delivery truck.

"Jesus, Martin. Pay attention! You nearly hit that truck." She glared at him. "I thought you said you were okay to drive."

"I'm okay," he muttered angrily. "I didn't see the light."

What a bitch she was! Beautiful, though. He'd have her and make her pay for it. She wanted him. Who wouldn't? He accelerated through the intersection, then slowed to a reasonable speed. They sat silent for a few minutes, then he asked, "Well, what kind of art do you like?"

She said nothing, then finally answered, "I've always liked the impressionists and the expressionists. Van Gough has always been a favorite."

"Dinosaur bones!" he said.

"I'm sorry?" she looked at him, miffed.

"True, the impressionists were the masters of their age, and Van Gough was a genius who is still somewhat relevant today, more as an inspiration for the young up-and-comers than anything else. He had a passion that he died for, and he was well ahead of his time. Time, however, marches on."

Martin was warmed by the power of his words. He tingled with a mastery that the drugs told him was his.

"What else do you like?"

"I like landscapes, I guess..."

"Landscapes," he laughed. "What else?"

She looked at him evenly. She didn't like the way the conversation had turned, but she continued. "I don't care too much for portraiture, and I've never seen much in most modern art, cubism or whatever else they call it. I don't know much about sculpture, to be honest with you. By your tone, I suppose whatever it is you're going to show me is, by your standard, what the world should consider great. It's not very often that I hear anyone claim the impressionists are dated. I know what I like. I know what speaks to me."

"Well, what makes you like something? What does it say to you?" he asked.

"I'm not sure what you mean."

"What is it that would make you spend time looking at a piece, or that would make you want to buy it and place it in your home?"

"I guess I would have to find it pretty or evocative..."

"That's what I'm looking for!" he almost shouted, slamming his hands down on the wheel.

"What, prettiness?"

"No, evocation! That's what lies behind all good art."

He was excited in his discussion and swerved to cut in front of another car just in time to barrel around the next corner.

"Slow down!" warned Amanda.

"Sorry."

He slowed.

"Evocation is the key. But not the evocation of the emotions, or the spirit or even of the rational mind. That's all garbage, sentimental rot. Art delves deeper than that. Today's art digs at the gut. It strikes the feral brute in man, what all of us keep locked up deep down within our psyche. If you look at something, and if it makes you sweat or scratch or retch, or if it makes you wet, then it's art. If it makes you do all of these things, why then, it's a masterpiece!"

He beamed at her in triumph, expecting a wowed response to his now famous theory.

"Hmm," she said. "I'll hold my judgment on that until I see your work."

She peered through the windshield.

Martin made his last turn and slowed as he neared the gallery. He spied two empty spaces, turned in sharply and managed to fill them both. He killed the engine and they climbed out of the car. Then taking her arm, he walked her up the steps.

"This is the Quadras gallery. We opened an exhibition of my new work here last night."

"Yes, you mentioned that at the restaurant. Aunt Emily said it would probably be an exhibition that I wouldn't soon forget."

"She's too kind."

Martin knocked on the heavy glass door. A security guard looked out, and upon recognizing him, unlocked the door and let them enter.

"Good evening, Mr. Drake. I didn't know you were coming."

"Oh, I forgot to call ahead, didn't I? I'm glad you're here. I didn't bring a key."

"I'm glad you're here too," said the guard in obvious relief. "This place gives me the creeps."

Martin smiled at that, and they walked past him into the gallery.

"Could we get some lights on in here?" he demanded.

"Yes, sir, just one minute."

As they stood in the dark, Amanda gazed out at the hulking shapes surrounding them. The gallery in shadows had an eerie feel.

With the magnetic clap of circuit breakers, the room came to life. Various horrors revealed themselves as the track lighting above them flashed on in random rows. Amanda started at the sight, but she regained her composure in an instant and calmly looked around.

"Come this way," said Martin.

He motioned her to follow. They stopped in front of "Crucifixion of a Martyr." It arched above them in its constant, ecstatic suffering. Martin stood for a moment in frowning contemplation. Then remembering, he bent down and flipped a switch at its base. With the whir of an electric motor, the plastic rats scratched to life, and blood began to drip down to their mechanical satisfaction.

"Power was off," he explained.

She looked at it for just a moment and then walked away to view another statue. She walked through the gallery quickly—too quickly, thought Martin. After encountering one sculpture, she turned and asked him, "Now what is this supposed to mean, Mr. Drake?"

He looked down at the one she was pointing to, "Assignation." It was a male mannequin decked out in patent leather bra and panties with a dog collar around his neck, dragging his chain behind him and sniffing the tail of a stuffed basset hound, which was sniffing his in return. The mannequin's hand squished down into a pile of plastic shit. He thought for a moment and answered, "I think this one speaks for itself."

"Yes, it does, doesn't it? I think I've seen enough. None of this would be appropriate for our new building. It's an office building, not a fun house. I do agree with you about your work, though, Mr. Drake. It does make one want to scratch and retch, but none of it made me—what was that other thing you said, oh yes—I'm afraid that none of it made me wet. What a pity.

"Sorry, but I think that I'll stick with the impressionists. Thanks for taking the time, but unfortunately we can't do business."

Martin stared at her in shock. What was he hearing? How could this woman not like his art? He was famous. He was a god. Oh well, all was not lost. He regrouped and said, "Well, Amanda, I guess cutting edge art has yet to slice through Cincinnati. Give us time. Sorry you didn't like my exhibition. I've done other things that you might find less shocking..."

"I don't believe that anything else you could do would shock me now, Mr. Drake."

He stalled for a second and then continued, "Why don't you let me buy you dinner?"

"I've already eaten, thank you."

"Well then, why don't you let me show you some of the hot spots around here?"

"No thank you, I really don't have the time." As she moved to the door, he followed her.

Sighing, he said, "Then I guess I'd better take you home."

"That's all right, don't bother. I'd rather take a cab. They're safer. Good night, Mr. Drake," she said with finality, and walked out the door to the street below.

The chemical power that had pulsed within him evaporated as he watched her go. Glumly, he walked back through his exhibit wondering what had gone wrong. He stood amid his statuary, turning on his heel to take it all in. The painted eyes of "Assignation" shined dully in the light. He looked into them and saw the chill he had seen in her eyes as she headed out the door. The eyes of the others were on him too: his other work, the priest, the billionaire, the girl in his bed. Ice crept up his spine. Martin turned and walked to the door. As he pushed through it, he caught his reflection in the glass. He ran down the steps and quickly drove away.

Chapter Seven

FATHER MANOEL STEPPED OUT of the Seafarers International House elevator door and was accosted by the gripes of seamen: "Then, I told that cocksucker, right there on the bridge with the pilot there with him, if he ever talked to me like that again, captain or not, I'd brain him and toss his fat ass right over the side....Oh, good morning, Padre. Didn't see ya coming."

The gray old men sat around a coffee table and looked up at the priest like children caught stealing a Sunday pie.

"Good morning, my friends," greeted Father Manoel in his Portuguese lilt. "Is everything okay?"

"Just great, Padre, another beautiful day in old New York," said the fat one.

The skinny one next to him grumbled, "I don't know how great it is with the union trying to cut back on our pension again. I didn't spend 35 years at sea bustin' my ass to end up in no damn poor house..."

"Quiet, Freddy. You don't need to go bitching at the Padre here. The union ain't gonna get nothin' off us, and you know it. Us pensioners got enough patrolmen in our pocket to carry off any vote. Now stop whining."

"You stop whining yourself, Alf, you stinkin' old potbellied..."

Alf shoved him and motioned up toward Father Manoel.

"Sorry," mumbled Freddy.

"Why don't you have a cup of coffee, Padre?" asked Alf. "Stay right there. I'll pour it myself."

"Thank you, that would be nice."

Alf hefted himself out of his chair and moved to pour from the coffee pot on the counter next to him. "You like sugar, Padre?"

"Yes, please. We Brazilians like our coffee sweet."

"So do us New Yorkers. Lots of sugar. Freddy there's from the South. He likes it stale and black. That's how come he's so skinny and mean."

Freddy looked at the table, saying nothing, like a nervous schoolboy in a principal's office. Father Manoel patted the frail old seaman on the shoulder and he seemed to relax a little.

"Cream?"

"No thanks."

Alf handed Father Manoel the coffee, which he accepted with a smile and a grateful sip.

"Has Reverend Blackwell come in yet?" asked the priest.

"Yes, sir, he was just here getting some coffee, and now he's in his office."

"Thanks, Alph."

Father Manoel walked across the lobby to the superintendent's office, a focus in this humble travelers' hotel known for its long history of harboring seafarers and clergy, and knocked on its open door.

"Come in," sounded a voice from the office.

The priest stepped inside, where he was greeted immediately by the aging pastor who rose to meet him.

"Good morning, Manoel. Are you off to do battle already?"

"Yes, I am. Ms. Quadras, the woman who owns the gallery I told you about, asked me to meet her at nine, so I thought I'd leave now. I don't want to be late."

"Late! It's barely seven o'clock. Sit with me and visit awhile. Have you had breakfast yet?"

"No, I only take coffee in the morning. Too much food for an old man makes a fat old man."

"Fat? Who's fat? I'm fat sure, but I always have been, except of course when I was down in the jungle with you. Nobody can stay fat, basting all day under that boiling sun, eating cassava roots and piranha day in and day out with never even the hope of a good old American hamburger and hot, greasy fries. I'm still surprised I survived that ordeal."

"I thought you liked mandioca and fish. You never complained back then."

"That was diplomacy, Manoel. I hope to never see one of those dreadful roots again."

The pastor motioned to his desk and to the two bagels stuffed with cream cheese sitting atop it.

"Now here's a breakfast, no scales, no teeth; you don't have to boil them to get the poison out. Come on and help me. I bought two when I shouldn't have bought any. Sit down here and keep a friend from dying of his vices. You know I don't need the cholesterol."

Father Manoel smiled and sat down. He took the bagel his friend offered him. It felt heavy in his hand. In the month he had spent in the U.S., he had never stopped marveling at the quantity of food Americans ate. This was truly the land of plenty, so much for everybody. Food, work and the chance of a future for all children, even the poor. One day maybe this miracle could pass to his country. That was his dream. He felt guilty eating in the morning. He didn't need to eat, and he thought of all of those he knew that did. Well, he couldn't mail it to them, could he? He bit into the warm bagel and tasted the cream cheese that filled his mouth with its abundance. It was wonderful—so much flavor.

"This is excellent, Barry. What do you call it?"

"It's a bagel. You don't know about bagels? How can a man who speaks English as well as you do, not know what a bagel is?"

"As I said, I don't eat in the morning, and besides we don't have these in Brazil." He took another bite. "They're dense but really good."

"Manoel, I can't get over how good your English is."

"It should be—you were the one who taught it to me."

"Oh yes! Remember all of those nights by the fire when we used to teach each other our languages, just so we could argue over religion? But that was over thirty years ago, and you weren't speaking this well then."

The rotund pastor licked the last remnants of his bagel from its wax paper wrapper. He cast a sidelong glance at the priest's bagel, but his friend didn't notice.

"Well, I've studied a lot since," Father Manoel said. "I read as much as I can. Did you know it's cheaper to buy imported American books than it is to buy their domestic translations? What a country we have, eh? I like to read the originals, anyway. They are always better. *Como está seu português*, Barry?"

"*Eu não falo mais português*. I'm afraid I lost it," said the pastor, a glimmer of remorse crossing his rosy face. "I just never had much chance to speak to anyone in Portuguese after I left Brazil. Occasionally a Brazilian or a Portuguese seaman shows up here to spend the night, but they're rare. I can still understand a few things, but I can't speak. I lost my Txukarramãe too, and there was so little of it to lose. Do you still keep in touch with the Indians?"

The priest looked pained. "No, no...not anymore."

Barry understood immediately that he had erred. He stood up, walked around the desk and clutched Father Manoel's shoulder with his chubby hand.

"Sorry, old friend. It was stupid of me to ask. I'm sorry."

Father Manoel gripped Barry's arm and looked up to him. The hurt passed quickly, and there was peace between them. He stood and smiled.

"Forget it, *amigo*. That was a long, long time ago."

Barry felt relief.

"I had better get going," said Father Manoel. "I don't want to be late. Barry, which train was that again, the number four?"

"Right, the four, five or six. They're all the same. Get off at 77th Street, and it will be just around the corner. Would you like me to walk you down to the station?"

"No, that's okay. I know where it is."

"Good luck then, Father. I'll pray for your success."

Father Manoel waved and walked out the door. As he stepped from the Seafarers International House, the New York winter struck his tropical soul with a cold and violent slap to the face. He shivered, pulled his coat closed at the lapels and walked briskly down the street to the subway station beneath Union Square. As he dashed across an intersection his foot crunched through the ice of a thin, curbside puddle. The sound of broken ice raised the hackles on his already goose-bumped neck. Ice, snow and freezing cold were part of God's mystery that he could do without. He rushed down the steps of the station into the teeming warmth of the racing crowd below. Upon reaching the turnstile, he stopped to pull his gloves off his frozen, uncooperative fingers so he could search his pockets for the tokens Barry had given him.

"Come on already! Get going or get out of the way," groused the man behind him in the complaining nasal twang that endeared New Yorkers to people all over the world.

Father Manoel stepped aside, and the line which had gathered so quickly behind him pushed past. His numb fingers struggled desperately through his many layered garb until they reached the pocket that held his tokens, trapped one and struggled to retrieve it from under his coat, where it seemed reluctant to leave its fleeting, woolly warmth.

With a drop of a token and a push of the turnstile, he was back in motion and moving down the tunnel to his train. He followed the signs and found his platform easily, and in minutes he was huddled in the press of humanity rolling uptown.

Glancing around, he was alone in his desire to look at others. The car was crammed with people of various types. Dark-suited, pasty-skinned businessmen lined the seats, intent on reading their newspapers and preserving their anonymity, all hoping to avoid the eyes of the many women standing above them. Young bohemians in greens, reds and blacks looked glumly to the floor as they held their ground against the mob, their outsized boots serving as anchors. High school kids clung in bunches, lost in a wild, raucous, profane language of their own.

All of these strange people and their strange talk began to awaken memories locked deep within him. The clack, clack, clack of the subway train became the slow, tack-tacking grumble of the river boat that had taken him up the Rio Xingu and deep into the heart of the forest many years before. He could see the sullen Indians and the stoic rubber tappers lying along the deck beneath the too small canopy, trying to find a spot in which to escape the oppressive noontime heat, and he could remember the hope and faith that battled with his fear. Fear that grew with every meter of passing river. He was to bring the word of God to the savage Xingu in a land that had claimed many before him, and which might claim many more. He prayed then, above the straining diesel, for the strength and love he'd need to carry out his mission, but he shuddered now with the memory of what had happened there.

Ave Maria sounded softly again and again into the somber crowd as Father Manoel prayed for a positive outcome in his dealings with the sculptor, for the future of the children in his care, for forgiveness and for another chance.

Chapter Eight

ARMINE LOOKED UP FROM her desk at the sound of knocking to see one of her salesmen standing at the door.

"What is it, Roger?"

"There's a priest here to see you, Ms. Quadras."

She looked at her watch and saw that he was half an hour early. *All the better*, she thought. *The sooner we get him in, the sooner we get him out, and the sooner we get our million.*

"Tell him I'll be right with him," she ordered curtly.

Roger nodded and left.

Armine put the receipts she had been checking in an ordered pile and slid them into her desk. She then stood and walked to a mirror on the wall to study herself. Her makeup was perfect, as always. She smiled at herself and her face changed from calculating business to flooding warmth; she broke the spell with a sly wink. *This shouldn't be that difficult*, she thought, and walked to the door.

"Good morning, Father Teixeira," she said, stepping out of her office and moving across the gallery to embrace the shivering priest. "Why look at you, Father. You're frozen. Come into my office and have some coffee. It will warm you up."

She took him by the arm and led him back the way she had come. As they walked, he looked at the sculpture surrounding them, which caused him to grimace and utter a silent prayer.

"Have a seat, Father, but first, may I take your coat?"

"No, if you don't mind, I'd rather keep it on. I'm still cold."

He clapped his gloved hands together and blew on them in an effort to warm them.

"Let me get you some coffee then." Armine moved to the pot she kept behind her desk, which was placed in such a way that it afforded whomever she was dealing with an unobstructed view of her backside as she turned to pour.

She cocked her head slightly and posed a question through the silky hair that half covered her face. "Sugar?"

"Please."

"Cream?"

"No, thank you."

She finished preparing two cups of coffee and returned to her desk. She slid one over to him and then slowly sat down in her chair.

"That should warm you up," she said, smiling.

"Thank you. Now what about the sculpture? You said that you had some pictures of Mr. Drake's work that might interest me."

He's right to the point, she thought. "Yes I do, one moment."

She got up slowly, letting her skirt rise high on her thighs before she brushed it back down. Then she sashayed over to a bookshelf and struggled to return with four large, bound albums. He rose and transferred the heavy pile from her arms into his own.

"Thank you," she murmured, feigning breathlessness. "They're rather heavy, aren't they? The life work of Martin Drake is pictured here."

She smiled as Father Manoel looked doubtfully at the books and set them on her desk.

"Let's begin here," she said, pushing an album in front of him. "This work dates from about ten years ago when Martin was heavily involved in, well, heavy metal." She chuckled, but her joke was lost on the priest, who just stared at her. "Well," she continued, "he did many abstracts in steel and wire, some of which are now very famous and valuable."

She stood close to him and brushed his shoulder with her hair as she reached to open the cover. The priest moved away from her and began to flip through the pages. He skimmed through the album quickly and then looked up to her.

"I don't understand this, Ms. Quadras. What is this supposed to mean? It's just a bunch of metal welded together in odd ways."

"They are abstractions, Father. I suppose they don't represent anything concrete..."

"I suppose that too. I won't allow him to weld a pipe on a steel plate and call it God. This won't do. What else can you show me? Hasn't he ever sculpted people or faces— something like that?"

"But Father," she instructed in a calming voice, "most of Mr. Drake's work is abstract. He tries to create forms that subtly convey meaning on an almost subconscious level..."

"Is that what he's doing out there with the blood and torture and carnality? What subtlety! This is nonsense," he said, pointing to the book.

"And that," he shot a finger out toward the gallery. "That is nothing more than, how do you say it? Oh yes. That is nothing but titillation! You can seriously call that art?"

He stared at her with a dark, questioning look.

A pained smile spread across her mouth as she replied, "To each his own, Father. Martin's work is controversial and not liked by everyone, but it is very highly regarded by all of the important critics."

"They must be sick or evil to foster the concept of this as art," Father Manoel said, then sat back and smiled blankly, refusing to be drawn out.

"Well then. You're not interested in his mannequin art or his steel abstractions." She picked up two of the albums and laid them aside. "But you might enjoy this."

She slid another album in front of him.

"These are the works of Martin's early bronze period."

Father Manoel opened the album and studied the pictures. He spent more time on these. They were bronze castings of various bent figures exhibiting human form and expression, though all bowed and in the throes of some type of internal agony. As he progressed through the images, however, he saw that the bronze castings became animal-like and contorted, in positions that defied empathy or understanding. The first few statues in the book had promise, though they seemed misdirected to the priest. They were not beautiful by any means, but Father Manoel saw the deft touch of a true sculptor. The man who had sculpted this early work had talent, that was obvious. After studying the book at length, he closed it and turned to face her.

"He is a capable artist, isn't he?" Father Manoel asked, delving deep into her eyes.

"Of course he is, Father Teixeira. He's Martin Drake."

"Call me Father Manoel. We Brazilians don't use last names very much."

"All right then, Father Manoel. He's famous all over the world."

He studied the woman standing before him, and Armine felt uncomfortable under his gaze. She liked male clients to look at her, to desire her, and she took pains to encourage it: it meant sales. But this wasn't the appraising stare of a man for a woman. His eyes probed hers, hunting for truth. She felt exposed and naked. Armine looked away and gathered the albums sprawled on her desk.

"I want to see him today," said the priest. "I want to talk to him. We might be able to work together after all."

"I'm sure that Martin would be delighted to meet with you, Father Teixeira…"

"Manoel."

"I'm sorry—Father Manoel. Yes, Martin would be delighted to see you, but unfortunately, he's not in the city today," she lied.

"Where is he? Doesn't he know that we have a million-dollar deal and not a lot of time to conclude it?"

Her mind spun. *Why did this man make her nervous? What was it about him? Quick, think of something*: "I apologize, Father, but today is Martin's day to teach. He runs a seminar for handicapped children upstate, and once a week he drives up to look things over and to teach the children art. He's such a dedicated man."

Father Manoel almost laughed at the thought of the dissipated sculptor doing anything for anybody. He knew she was lying, but he also knew that it was useless to accuse her of it. He pretended to accept the lie and asked, "Well then, will he be back tomorrow?"

"Oh yes. I'm sure he'll be up early, busy working on your project. You know how obsessed artists can be." She let out a chuckle, which she immediately regretted.

"Good, my daughter, that's wonderful. I'd like to visit his studio then, tomorrow morning. I'd like to talk over our commission with him. Maybe this time tomorrow?"

She swallowed and said, "That would be fine, Father. Let me give you his studio address."

She sat at the desk and copied it down quickly on a sheet of paper.

He took it from her, rose and said, "Thank you, my daughter. It's been an interesting morning. Please, if you have a chance to speak to Mr. Drake, tell him that I am very excited about our project. It means so much to the children: a chance of an education! I'm sure that he will understand, as he is an educator himself."

A shudder passed through her when he bent down and kissed her on the cheeks before departing. She waved lamely as he left, realizing this wouldn't be as easy as she'd thought. When he was gone, she picked up the telephone and dialed it. It rang several times before it was answered.

"Yeah?"

"Vicki, it's Armine."

"Hi, sweetmeat, finally decided to take a walk on the wild side?"

"Cut it out, Vicki, I don't have much time."

Armine had been shaken by the priest, though she didn't know why, and didn't feel like playing word games with a dyke who'd find it difficult to mate on any side of the sex spectrum.

"You remember our meeting, don't you?" she asked.

"How could I forget a meeting with you? I've been masturbating for weeks."

Armine let it pass.

"Good. Listen, Vicki, I need you to do me a favor. I'm going to be out of the office all morning, and my cell phone's on the blink. I need you to call Martin, wake him up and make sure he shows up for our meeting this afternoon. It's important."

"I'll make sure he's there, lover. I've worked out a whole new concept that he just has to see. I'm creaming to do it, but I need the boss man's approval."

"Thanks, Vicki. I'll see you at four." She hung up and gathered her coat. As she headed out the door, she felt—for one of the few times in her life—that she wasn't the one in control.

Chapter Nine

"WHY, MARTIN, HERE YOU are already, only forty minutes late," said Armine wryly. She was seated at her desk with Vicki, where they were looking over a large pile of sketches.

Martin smiled as he walked in and took a seat. "Hello, girls," he said, putting an arm around Vicki and blowing Armine a kiss from across the desk. "Are we having fun yet?"

"I always have fun with Armine, Martin. You know that. Not as much fun as I'd like to have but give me time. I'll break the door down yet." The fat, greasy woman pouted her lips and blew Armine a kiss of her own.

Armine reacted with a slight, snide crinkle of the lip and eye.

"Well, what are we looking at here?" said Martin as he picked up a drawing. It was a mannequin caught in yet another turn of Vicki's vicious fancy. He picked up several more drawings and sorted through them, all variations on the same perverse theme. He pulled two out of the stack and put them aside. When he was done with the rest, he studied the two and then held them up to Armine, who shook her head "no."

"Tone these two down a bit, Vick," he instructed as he handed the sketches back to her. "The rest are great as always, you twisted little soul."

He pinched her cheek.

She blushed and looked to her shoes, then burst out with, "That's old stuff, guys. Wait 'til you see this!"

She reached into a bag and pulled out two small terra-cotta figures, which she carefully handed to Martin. "Aren't they great?"

They were two little Indians locked in a grunting embrace. Their massive organs meshed into each other as Martin rocked them in his hands.

"Careful, or you'll break off his prick."

Vicki took the figures from him and set them down on the pile of her designs. There they lay, oblivious to spectators, lost in their eternal rut.

"They're Peruvian. I bought them yesterday in a junk shop down in The Village." She beamed at the others, awaiting a response.

"That's very nice, Vick. I'm glad to know that Peruvians have the same hobbies we do. Kind of makes one feel universal, doesn't it?" Martin squeezed her arm.

"What do you think, Armine?" Vicki asked.

"I think we'd better stick to mannequins."

"Hold on. Just wait until you see this." Vicki reached into her sketch case and pulled out three more drawings, which she placed on the desk beside her grunting inspirations. Martin and Armine leaned over to study them. The first was a couple in a struggling clinch, wrapped tightly together in barbed wire, both crowned with barbed wire laurels.

Vicki surveyed their faces and explained, "I can make them in clay to keep costs down, and the barbed wire will work well with clay. I can wrap them when they're still soft, so the barbs really dig in."

Martin flipped to the next one: a male contortionist rolled in a back-breaking act of autoeroticism that pubescent boys could only dream of. He smiled and flipped to the last sketch: a reclining woman massaging her breasts and reaching down to her nether-regions with a serpentine tongue of bullfrog proportions. He looked up at Vicki, who was prepared to make her pitch.

"What I'm getting at here is that all sexual relationships stem from our inability to take care of our own needs."

She pointed to the figures groping each other in the barbed wire. "We're trapped into closeness with each other as a means of getting off. Think how much better life would be if we were only more limber!"

She winked at Armine and then blushed again when Martin started mussing her hair.

"My little philosopher," he cooed, but thought: *How sick you are and how rich you make me.* He kissed her forehead, and she grinned bashfully down to the desktop.

"Work on it, Vicki," said Armine. She started to organize the clutter atop her desk. "But right now, continue with the mannequins. I'll be ready for another twenty in two weeks."

"That's easy, the others can do the mannequins while I work on these. Speaking of the others," she turned to Martin. "Armine told me that you were gonna come down to the studio and talk to those assholes. They're always whining, asking about you, when you're gonna come in and all, and they don't like taking orders from me. Some of them are grumbling about quitting, saying that they came to work to learn from you, not to slave away for me on cook's wages. I'd be glad to see them go, personally, but I can't meet deadlines without worker bees, can I?"

"You didn't talk to your artists yet?" Armine frowned and shot Martin an incriminating look.

"No, I didn't have a chance."

"What the hell did you do all day? All you had scheduled was your little tryst with Deborah."

Vicki smiled knowingly. Martin stared her down and then responded, "I brought someone here last night to look at our stuff. She was looking for sculpture to decorate a building, but I guess this wasn't what she was looking for."

He sighed upon remembering.

"Well, at least you were working at a sale. Good. But get over to the studio and placate those artists. If you don't spend a little time stroking those guys, they'll quit, and we'll just have to hire more who you'll have to train all over again. You really want to have to do that? Anyway, we don't have the time right now. What have you come up with, for the Banks contract?"

Martin shrugged his shoulders.

"You haven't thought about it?"

"I was busy. Anyway, talk to Vicki about it. She's the one who's going to do the job."

"What job?" asked Vicki.

"Martin and I closed an important contract for a new piece at the exhibition opening, and we need to start work on it immediately."

Armine picked up the figurines on her desk, handed them back to Vicki and said, "Put your friends on ice awhile. I want you to get started on this."

"What is it?" asked Vicki, as she took her little statues and carefully slid them into her bag.

"We need to do a bronze bust..."

"You're going to let me cast in bronze? Gee, it must be big if you're willing to pop for bronze."

"It has to be bronze," said Armine, ignoring her gibe, "a bronze bust of the face of God."

Vicki put her bag down and sat back in her chair. Her eyes glistened with the rumbling machinations of a mind full of broken but sharp-toothed cogs.

"I want ideas from you on this too, Martin. You both need to have something sketched out by tomorrow morning."

"Tomorrow morning?" gaped Martin.

"That's right. That priest was in here today within minutes of opening. He looked through everything you've done and didn't like any of it, but he did seem a bit interested in your earlier bronze work. He wanted to talk to you today, but I covered for you and said you were out of town. He wants to deal with you directly, not with me. He's insistent, Martin, and I don't think that he will be easy to put off. You two are meeting with him at nine tomorrow morning at the studio."

"You're crazy. I don't even wake up until noon. Vicki can handle it."

"Martin, he asked for you, and I said you'd be there."

"Forget it. I'll be in bed."

"Vicki," asked Armine, "would you excuse us? Martin and I need to talk. Be ready with ideas and drawings about this bust tomorrow morning. Get some of the others working on it if you need to. I want this done as quickly as possible."

"Sure, sweetmeat. I'll have something for you tomorrow," said Vicki, gathering up her sketches.

"And Vicki…"

Vicki looked up.

"Nothing too wild. This is for a priest. It has to be reasonable. He wants the face of God, not the Marquis de Sade."

Vicki smiled upon hearing that the client was a priest. *This could be fun*, she thought. She nodded, put the sketches in her case and got up to leave. Just as she opened the door to walk out, she called behind her to Martin, "See you bright and early, boss."

Martin grumbled and slumped deeper in his chair. When the door closed, Armine stood up and laid into him, "A million dollars, Martin, a *million* dollars, almost for free. That buys a lot of whiskey, doesn't it? And you don't have to do a damn thing for it either, other than to show up once in a while, gladhand that priest and pretend you're interested. What's so hard about that?"

Martin sat sullenly in his chair, saying nothing.

"What's the matter with you? You should be jumping at this. It's the biggest deal we've ever made for a single piece, and now when I need you to clinch it, you act like a spoiled child." Armine scowled down at him, anger flashing in her eyes.

Martin looked up. He wanted to tell her that the priest had gotten to him, that he felt as if the priest had managed to somehow cut through his layered exterior to see him as he truly was, which was maddening enough, but it was more than that: he felt that the priest somehow wanted to make him pay. He wanted to tell her. He wanted to talk to somebody and she was his best friend, not that he could really count on her in a crisis, but she was the only friend he really had anymore—other than Vicki, who couldn't possibly understand. Armine would be understanding. She'd listen. He opened his mouth to speak, but froze at what he saw in her eyes. They were all there: the priest, Banks, the girl in his bed, Amanda, and now Armine, all boring into him, accusing him. He rose quickly, grabbed his coat and growled to Armine as he left her office, "You take care of it, Armine. I've got the name. Now you go market it and let Vicki do the work."

As he walked toward the gallery door, she chased after him.

"All right, Martin. All right. I'll take care of it, but you need to come back here. We're not done. We need to discuss payroll and sales figures."

"Later."

He walked outside into the traffic noise that rumbled through the waning light of the frigid afternoon.

Chapter Ten

A N INCOMPREHENSIBLE MESSAGE MUMBLED from the intercom into the seething mass below it, and in an instant the subway doors opened with a swoosh. Father Manoel was straining to see if this was his stop, but since he was standing near the door, he was pushed through it instantly by the impatient crowd that teemed forth. He struggled against the tide until he saw the plaque that marked the stop as Broadway, then he relaxed and let the rushing flow wash him up to the street. The cold wind dug into his summer bones as he gained the surface, causing him to shrug down into his collar while he gathered his bearings. He looked up and then down Broadway, trying to read a street name he would recognize, and which would tell him the way to walk. It was more difficult down here. He was below the disciplined ranks of numbered streets that made New York easy for tourists, and now he was entering the warren of lower Manhattan, where streets meandered lazy as rivers and where unseasoned foreigners could freeze to death searching for a kind local with the key to unlock the mystery of the address they sought.

Father Manoel was amazed at the number of rude citizens who rebuffed him when he asked for the simplest of information. He, who was dressed as a priest! He couldn't fathom how shop clerks, who more or less had to respond to a plea from the lost, could be totally ignorant and bereft of information about the very street on which they worked. A Brazilian would spend an hour chatting with you, only to let you know, in the end, that he had no idea where you were trying to go. He then might advise you to give up looking—better instead to stay awhile longer and share in a bottle of cachaça and more conversation. Here, though, people were different. They wouldn't even look at you.

He unfolded the Xeroxed map of the area that Barry had given him and looked to the highlighted street at the head of the little yellow trail that scribed his journey—Walker Street. He strained to see the closest street sign, but it was too distant. With a shrug, he walked toward it. Howard Street. Wrong again. He always picked the wrong direction. He turned and walked back quickly, chattering aloud the names of passing streets and counting them against the ones marked on the map that shivered in his hands.

Today he would meet with the artist who had offended him the night they met, and who, in a way, offended him even more now. His visit to the gallery the day before had been a mixed blessing. The catalogues of Drake's art were, for the most part, depressing. Except for his early bronzes. They were grotesque, and clearly they were manifestations of an angry psyche straining for truth ever-further in the wrong direction. But there was something else to those bronzes: although they were ugly and malformed, they showed something more—a tremendous raw talent. Only a genius could have sculpted them. In their screaming contortions and in their broken, twisted limbs lay the barren seeds of beauty. He, who could create them, could create things of wonder. That is, if he wanted to. All the rest of the catalogued art, though, was nothing but junk—junk that would remain wholly un-picked lying in a heap in the poor, mean streets of Rio or São Paulo, except perhaps by a scrap-metal monger. Rubbish.

Father Manoel quickened his pace when he spied Worth Street and hurried down it, escaping the cutting wind that roared up Broadway.

He knew now that Martin Drake wasn't just a twisted incompetent who somehow managed to talk himself into respectability and wealth. He knew that Drake was a fraud. He was talented—that was obvious in his bronzes. The question was, why didn't he use the talent given him, and why, if he was truly warped, did he shock in mediocre measure when a man of his ability could probably be incredibly shocking and even more offensive, if he only chose to be? He pondered this. Maybe Martin Drake was just lazy.

Laziness was a sin that he could not, and would not, tolerate. None of the children in his program were allowed to achieve less than they were capable of. It didn't matter if he got them late, past the age of normal matriculation— that was not uncommon in a country where three-year-olds worked the streets alone, panhandling for the food their families could not provide them. His teachers would instruct a twelve-year-old how to read, enroll him in school and keep him there until he graduated, if he was willing to put forth his maximum effort. Effort led to learning, and learning opened the wellspring of intelligence and ability that could free a spirit from the chains that bound it in whatever circumstance it was thrust into at birth. He cried at night to think of the children in his care who tried so hard for the chance of a life that the people of this cold country, where he now walked, could only find to be pitifully substandard. But he knew that God, in his wisdom, made life a struggle and that the future was built on foundations laid today. Someday maybe his children, or more realistically, their children's children might build beautiful cities such as this. That was his dream.

The opulence of Armine's gallery galled him. It seemed to him a pagan temple, brightly gilt and bereft of spirit, so different than the favelas where he worked, muddy cities of redbrick and tin that buzzed with song and laughter, and with the rhythm and joy of life. Maybe wealth wasn't such a great gift. Let them have their million dollars, he prayed, but help us get the assistance we need to run our crèches. He thought of the boys and girls who were to graduate from high school this year. They would be the first from his program to finish school. Their faith in the program and in themselves had led them so far. He prayed he would be able to work with the sculptor to ensure that their years of work would finally be rewarded. *Senhor Jesus, grant them this*, he prayed. Nagging fears from his Indian days on the Xingu burst up to the surface of his memory, shattering his calm and obscuring the picture of his future graduates. *God, please let me get it right this time.*

Father Manoel stopped to check the address Armine had given him, 1185 West Worth. This was it. Relief swept through him as he opened the door and began to climb up the warm stairs and out of the cold. Number 316, the Drake studio, was the first door he encountered when he stepped off the third-floor landing. Actually, it was the only working door on the third floor's south side. All of the others led to the same gigantic area that the studio occupied, but they were all locked and boarded shut and further blocked by work benches, machines and stacks of art supplies. Grinding and clamor sounded through the door. It sounded like a factory. Father Manoel knocked, but no one answered. He knocked again, this time much harder. The noise subsided for an instant, and someone shouted to another that somebody was at the door. A moment later it swung open.

"Yeah?" uttered a greasy woman in a black shapeless frock dusted with fiberglass.

"I'm Father Manoel."

He looked at her and then glanced at the numbers tacked to the door to make sure he was at the right place. He was.

"I'm here to see Mr. Drake about a sculpture."

"Oh, hi. Come on in. I'm Vicki."

She turned and walked back to a drafting table centered on their side of the large work area. He shut the door and followed her. The studio was populated by six young men whose work went on unabated. Grinders whirred and spit sparks and dust into the air, particles highlighted by the intermittent blue flash of an arc welder that buzzed across the room.

Vicki closed-in on the priest and spoke above the noise into his ear. "Martin's not here, but he told me you were coming in this morning to talk about a sculpture—you're the face of God guy, right?"

"Yes, I am, but I had an appointment with Mr. Drake..."

"What?"

He shouted to be heard, "I have an appointment to see Mr. Drake."

"He's not here. I'll handle it."

"This is very important. I must speak to Mr. Drake personally about his work."

Vicki held her hand up in a signal to wait and then turned to scream across the room, "Hey! Hey! You two over there."

The grinding died as the men looked around to see who was yelling.

"Hey, knock off the grinding for a while. I'm talking over here. Go work on something else."

The men put down their grinders and pondered the steel angles they were shaping, wondering what they could do with them that wouldn't make noise. They gave up, got up and moved to a work bench piled high with the limbs and disembodied heads of a dozen mannequins, which they then began to sift through. As they shifted the heap, a head broke loose from the top of it and bounced and rolled across the dirty tiles. It came to rest at Father Manoel's feet, staring up at him with lifeless eyes from under a broken forehead.

Vicki yelled to the men who sent it. "Careful, assholes. You ruined this one!" She booted it back to them. "Keep it up, and you'll start paying for your fuck-ups."

She turned back to Father Manoel, "Like I said, Martin's not here, but he told me to handle your project."

"I don't understand this. We had an appointment to meet this morning. I don't have much time for delay. When do you think he will be in?"

"He might come in this afternoon around three or four. He's supposed to come down and straighten out these goons I have to work with, but I don't know if he'll make it. We don't see much of him at all, unless he comes down here to sign the pieces or to check a shipment."

"This is his studio?"

"That's what they tell me."

"Well then, how can he not come here? Where does he sculpt?"

Vicki laughed. "The only thing that Martin sculpts these days is a hangover. That's not the way it works. He doesn't actually do the work. We do. Martin and I work out the designs, and then I build them with the help of these idiots. Hell, I did all the designs for the last two lines myself. Martin and I traded ideas on it, but the work was mine."

"You mean to tell me that you did all of the work for that exhibition at the Quadras gallery ?"

"That's right. There's nothing wrong with that. Most of the public knows Martin doesn't do the grunt work anymore. It's pretty standard practice. Da Vinci had helpers too, you know."

"But they were apprentices. He taught them a trade. He didn't steal their talent. He enhanced it. Why do you let him do this to you?"

"Listen pal, I like what I do. Martin gets the glory, sure. Let him have it. I like to create things, and he lets me do it, whatever I want. And anyway, do you know how many starving artists there are out there? Thousands. Without a name like Martin's to work under, I'd be waiting tables during the day and working on my art at night whenever I had enough cash to pop for supplies. Hey, this job doesn't pay that great, but it's solid and steady, and it's what I want to do."

"How can it not pay well? We're paying a million dollars for this bust, and he expects you to do all of the work. He's getting rich off of your labor."

Vicki's eyes glazed at the mention of the million dollars. She stared blankly at the large priest and scratched idly at the roll of fat that bulged out beneath her saggy breasts. She had no idea how much her work was selling for. She never asked. The work was the important thing. Martin paid her around $40 thousand a year—it varied depending on how much overtime she worked—and although forty grand didn't go very far in New York City, she never complained. She had always considered herself lucky. But a million dollars for one piece? Martin and Armine were using her, and she had always thought them friends, partners really, three comrades doing what they loved to do, doing what they believed in. Now she knew the truth. She was no partner. She was shit, just another studio idiot, maybe the dumbest of them all. She felt betrayed.

She looked up at Father Manoel annoyed that he knew what she should have known all along. For now, she'd have to let it go, for now...

"Look, I don't care about that. I just want to do my work and be left alone. So do you want to see my designs or what?"

"Why not," he responded, knowing full well that nothing the true creator of Martin Drake's mannequins would design could be of any interest to him. "Then I want to talk to Mr. Drake. Where can I find him?"

"Probably in bed. He usually sleeps 'til noon. Now come over here."

She led him to an easel. He looked and at once was incensed at what he saw: it was one of the autoerotic designs she had shown Martin the day before.

On seeing his reaction, she felt a pleasure, a sense of satisfaction. *You're just jealous*, she thought. *Not so limber, are you Father?*

"Take it easy. That's not one of yours: they're still in my case. I took them home last night to finish them, stayed up all night to do it. Just one second."

As she moved to fetch her case, they heard a knock on the door. She walked over to open it.

"Oh, hi Armine."

"Good morning, Vicki. Has Father Manoel come in yet?"

She saw him as soon as she asked, so she waltzed over to greet him with the click, click, click of high heels on hard tile.

"Good morning, Father Manoel! How are you today?" She kissed him on both cheeks in the manner she knew some foreigners kissed each other. He returned the kisses, but his were tentative, without the goodwill his pecks normally conveyed.

"Mr. Drake is not here," he stated flatly.

"Oh yes, I know. He just called me. It seems as if he was involved in a minor car accident on his way back from his seminar. Remember? The one I told you about yesterday."

He looked at her but said nothing.

Armine looked to Vicki, who had returned with her sketch case.

"Vicki, could you please show us the designs for the face of God bust that Martin couriered to you yesterday afternoon?"

"The one's he couriered to me?"

"That's right, dear. You *know*, the sketches I told you to have ready for us to view this morning."

Vicki looked blank for a moment and then slowly handed over her sketch case. *What the fuck,* she thought. *Armine and Martin are making all the money off this, not me. If she wants to get caught lying to this guy, then screw her. I just work here.*

Armine took the case, withdrew the sketches and placed them on the easel before looking at them. This, she instantly regretted. Laughing back at them in mocking heartlessness was the visage of a fat, debauched woman with the beginnings of a mustache traced across her fleshy upper lip and leaves sprouting out from her hairy ears.

Armine looked at it, dumbfounded. *Now what was she going to do?* Father Manoel glanced at the sketch, shook his head in disbelief and then turned to glare darkly at Armine. She smoothed her skirt, wiping the sweat from her palms as she did.

"Well," she chuckled, "this obviously doesn't belong here."

She pulled it from the stack only to reveal another, more chilling aspect of the same woman.

"I don't understand this. Martin must have erred and sent the wrong sketches."

"Drake didn't draw those sketches!" roared the priest. He pointed to Vicki. "She did!"

"Oh, I didn't know. All right, Vicki, where are the sketches that Martin sent?" She crossed her arms smugly, and hoped desperately that Vicki would play along and somehow get them out of this. Vicki shrugged and looked away.

"He sent no sketches, Ms. Quadras. He had no car wreck and he never left the city. You've been lying to me."

Armine flushed with the ironic, righteous anger that wells within the guilty when they are caught red-handed.

"I'm sure I don't know what you mean," she managed to breath out sweetly, though she didn't feel sweet at all.

"*Mentira!* You know exactly what I mean. You've been lying to me all along. Drake doesn't run an art seminar for children. What kind of parents would send their child to something like that? He's sleeping it off in his apartment, isn't he? Now tell me where he lives."

"I can explain, Father..."

"Enough! I have no more time for you—or for this." He swept his hand in an arc around him. "Now give me his address or forfeit your contract. Give it to me. Now!"

Armine's smile pained her, but she held it up to camouflage the spite that swelled inside her. Her thin lips pulsed with malice, but she couldn't let them speak. She had to remain calm and nonreactive. The damage was done. Now she had to turn it around. *All right,* she thought. *Martin's got me into this. Let him get me out of it. I'll work*

on Banks, but Martin can have this pissy priest all to himself.
She shrugged, let down her smile and opened her purse. She
pulled out her date book and scribbled Martin's address on
one of the pages, which she ripped out and handed to the
priest.

Father Manoel glanced at it, then walked toward the door.

"Wait, Father, wait!" yelled Vicki. "Don't you want to
see what it is I'm getting at here? It's like an Earth Mother
theme."

He didn't answer and was soon out of view, booming
down the stairs.

"Vicki," hissed Armine icily, "do you have any idea how
important this contract is to us?"

"Hey, don't look at me like that. It's not my million. I
get paid by the hour."

Vicki walked away from her, picked up a grinder and
filled the room with a screaming cloud of iron sparks and
burning embers.

Chapter Eleven

A SHARP, STACCATO RAP SOUNDED at the edge of consciousness. What was it? *Nothing. Go back to sleep.* Martin rolled over and buried his head beneath a pillow. He drifted away, but was brought back by the incessant rapping that grew even more intense. *Shit.* His head began to throb with the rapping. The throbbing he knew; it was with him every morning now, the hangover with which he rang in his day, but coffee, Advil and his breakfast shot usually took care of it, unless he had gone wild the night before and really had to pay. But what was this other thing? *Oh. The door. Someone's knocking on the door.* He dug in deeper beneath his pillow, but the noise was still there, now louder. Whoever it was, wasn't going away.

"Damn," he cursed furrily. He got up and shuffled to the door, which was beginning to sound like a drum. He squinched through the peephole. Whoever was making the racket was too close to see, just another ball of fuzz like the one squashed inside his skull.

"Who is it?" he shouted.

The pounding stopped.

"Father Manoel. We had a meeting this morning, remember? Now let me in."

This time of morning, a quarter to eleven, was dream time for Martin, though he seldom dreamed anymore. But, dream time or not, his hangover and sleepiness couldn't dull the memory of the man behind the door. He knew exactly who it was without having to search through the fog. *I should have stayed in bed*, he thought, *but now there was nothing to be done.* He had to open the door and talk to this man who stood between him and his million dollars. Martin unlatched his many locks and swung the door open.

"What time is it?" he asked the angry priest, who already was pushing his way into the living room.

"It's almost eleven. We had a meeting at nine. Why didn't you come?"

"I told Armine yesterday that I couldn't make it..."

"Why not?" interrogated the priest. "Do you have to sleep until noon every day? Are you sick? Don't you do anything?"

Martin didn't respond, but instead mumbled, "Just a second, I've got to drink some water and make some coffee."

"Forget the coffee," growled the priest. "You should have had it hours ago. Now let's talk about my sculpture."

He seethed with ire and authority, overwhelming the sleepy man with stern determination. Not knowing quite why, Martin forsook his coffee and led Father Manoel across the living room and into his private studio. He shuffled to his sculpting table, which was centered in the room, and sagged onto a stool where he cradled his thumping head and squinted up at the priest with red, tired eyes.

"Have you thought about our sculpture?" demanded the priest, towering above him, hands on hips.

"Sure, I've thought about it."

"Well?"

"Oh, I don't know. I'm not done thinking yet. Why don't you meet me down at the factory, I mean my other studio, in about a week. We can talk about it then."

"I don't have a week! And I just came from your factory where your assistant showed me the ideas she created and that you intended to palm-off on me. God as some ludicrous, androgynous fiend? Do you really wish to be known as the man who created such an image of God?"

"I don't know," Martin confessed. "I didn't get a chance to look at her sketches, but I doubt it would make much difference to me. If there is a God, surely, he can take a joke. Look around you, Father—the world is full of God's comedy."

Martin's head pounded, and he wished the priest would go away.

Father Manoel ignored the jab, sat down next to the artist and studied him. Maybe reason would work with this man. Why not? They had to come to an understanding, and they both knew it. So why the problem? *I should be more civil,* he thought. *Maybe that would help.*

He calmed himself and spoke in a normal tone, "Listen to me, Mr. Drake. I've seen your work, all of it in pictures. I'll be honest with you: most of what you've done seems nothing but a travesty to me. I don't know you, but it seems as if you're moving farther and farther toward the irreverent and the ridiculous just to see how far you can go, to see how far you can lead people and to see how gullible they could possibly be. It's as if you are making a joke, not out of your subjects, but out of your patrons."

Martin looked at him and quietly wondered how this man, of all people—this thick-accented zealot from third-world slums half a world away—could read him like none of his sophisticated critics could. This priest could see where others were blind. He seemed almost comical in his frayed black coat and the ski gloves he had yet to take off, as if he were the country bumpkin in one of those old comedies who takes a trip to the big city and suddenly finds himself the brunt of all jokes. Like those bumpkins, he somehow turned the tables on his detractors with subtle, native skill. Three days ago, Martin could not have imagined being even remotely involved with a South American priest in any way, but now he found himself plagued by the accusation in this man's eyes—whether the priest was with him or not. Worse, he found himself under the priest's thumb. It was Father Manoel who was calling the shots. Martin tried dodging him for days by putting slippery smooth Armine in his path, and now where was he? In Martin's home studio, mid-morning, critiquing his work.

As Martin awoke, latent nausea rose from the pit of his sour gut to his throat and throbbing temples. He couldn't allow this man to get the better of him. It was irrational. Millionaires and aristocrats were malleable, soft clay in his hands. Why wasn't this priest? He would have to try to put a stop to this. Martin had to get the upper hand, but for some reason, he didn't think he could. When he fought against the priest he felt as if he fought against himself, but he had to do it. He couldn't let this eat at him any longer. Feeling as trapped and angry as a field mouse caught beneath a tabby's paw, he instinctively lashed back, futile though it seemed.

He took a deep breath, hardened himself and then responded, "Look, Father, I'm one of the most famous sculptors in this country. And you? Who are you? Some no-name missionary from Brazil up here begging for money to haul back home for who knows what. Why bother? The largess of America has been pouring into countries like yours for over two hundred years. Are they any better off?

The countries, I mean, not the individual beggars. The money goes somewhere, but never it seems, to those who need it. The world will always be peopled by the poor. Do you really think that you can make a difference? I doubt it, but then I don't care either.

"I don't care who you are or what you do with your money. That's not my business, and I won't presume to judge you. Now extend me the same courtesy. We have to work together, no matter how uncomfortable that might be for both of us, because it's the desire of Harry Banks, and he's the man with the money we both want. Let's try to work together and get this thing done, so we can both get what we want. But don't judge me or dictate to me because I won't take it. I don't have to.

"Who needs the money more, me or you? I'd like it, sure, but I could do just fine without it. What about you? Do you really want to let this money go? If these schools, or whatever it is you run, are so damn important to you, wouldn't you do better to go back to my studio, work something out with Vicki and leave me the hell alone? You'll get your sculpture on time that way. That's the way I operate. You're not doing either of us any good by being here, so why don't you just go."

"I'm sorry, my son, but I'm afraid I can't do that."

Father Manoel saw the difference between them then, the thing that separated the two. It was faith. Not the religious faith in deity, but the faith in one's self. Father Manoel had it, that was why he battled for his kids. That was why he was here now. He wasn't absolutely sure that his work would make a difference in the world, but he thought it could, God willing. And he knew he had to try. Faith was the key, and this man didn't seem to have any. It was as if, for some reason, he had given up and now was content to watch his life roll by while he sat back and laughed cynically at its passage. Father Manoel remembered the dark days when he had lost his own faith and how hard it was to regain it. *Maybe that is why I'm here*, he thought. *Perhaps I've been sent to help this man.* Martin was now illuminated before him in a light of understanding. He was the man that Father Manoel could have become if hadn't regained the path. He looked to Martin without a trace of anger. His eyes were placid. They reflected sincerity.

"Listen to me, Mr. Drake. If your assistant could do the work, I would be more than happy to let her, believe me, but she can't. I don't think that she is capable. I've talked to her and have seen what she does. Her vision's twisted. Something's not right about her, like she's living in some parallel world or seeing this one through gray, myopic eyes. She could never sculpt something worthy of consecration. If I go to her, we will argue for two months and come up with nothing. The deadline will pass. Then I will have to close my children's centers, and you will lose your money. She's not capable of helping us. But you are. I know it. I've seen pictures of your early bronzes. They are chilling and awful, but they are good for what they are, and they are honest. They show your struggle, Mr. Drake, and are admirable for that, and you are admirable for struggling to create them. Please, work on this for me. The hopes of many people hinge on this sculpture. Make something beautiful that will be a worthy tribute to God. Please help us. Help the children. You know you can."

Anxiety stirred within Martin. He had been staring down at a lump of clay lying on his worktable while the priest spoke, and now he wondered how long it had been since he'd touched it. The clay had been there for ages, and he didn't want to touch it. Had that ever gotten him anywhere in life? Those bronzes, the ones the priest was ranting about, had cost him their weight in sweat…and for what? Only a fraction of them sold, and they didn't sell for much. It was always that way. He had poured his soul into his sculpture when he was young, trying to imbue it with a spirit and soul of its own that would turn it from dull, lifeless material into an animate symbol of that for which it stood. And what was the payment for his struggle? Obscurity, poverty and scorn from the few critics who even bothered to notice him.

Martin had decided long ago to give up his painful struggle and to mimic the current successes of the day. Shortly thereafter, he was considered the best and brightest of the lot. Recognition, wealth and fame were his. Did he sell himself out? *Sure.* Was the price of this life the loss of the soul that had once burned so bright within him? *Maybe.* He wasn't sure about that. He wasn't sure about anything anymore, other than the stupidity of those who now proclaimed his genius. But what did it matter? He no longer had to suffer the taunts and petty gibes of the critics who belittled the work he battled so hard to create. Who was laughing at whom these days? No, he wouldn't try to go back and capture what had dwelled within him once. It was gone. It was dead. He was now what he had made himself: Martin Drake, socialite, wit, purveyor of illusions—and total, utter failure.

This priest had known that immediately, even before they had met. Good for him. There was at least one man alive with decent aesthetic sense. But if he knew Martin to be a phony, why was he pushing him so hard? Was he some sort of New Age alchemist who strove to conjure gold from the shards of broken dreams? Well, it wouldn't work, not this time. The priest would just have to take what he could get from Vicki and run with the money. A million dollars wasn't really worth the pain. Why couldn't this priest just let it go?

Martin looked up at Father Manoel and spoke in a tired voice. "Father, I thought you understood me. You had me figured out the moment we met. It was written in your eyes. You thought I was a fraud, and you were right. I'm no better than Vicki. In fact, I'm worse. My art's dead, so now I profit on hers. If you think you can somehow convert me or change me, forget about it. You're much too late. If you don't want to work with Vicki, fine. I really don't need the money. Now please, leave me in peace."

"Please, Mr. Drake, do this for us. You know you can, I beg you..."

"Get the fuck out of here."

"Let me help you with this."

"I said get the fuck out!"

Father Manoel sighed and started to get up. Maybe he was wrong. Maybe Mr. Drake was too far gone after all. As he stood, he glanced across the studio, wondering if this was indeed the end of their road together. Then he saw something that stunned him.

There was a statue of a woman centered on the far wall, which was free of the clutter that festooned the others, as if it were a sacred place, a temple that was hers alone. He had never seen anything like her. She was walking away from them into the infinite whiteness of the wall, but had turned back for one last look. He moved closer to get a better view. She was crying desperate tears, and her face, wreathed by soft bronze locks, bore a tortured look. It was as if she was leaving someone whom she loved with all her heart, but could no longer bear to live with. Her sad eyes swam in a sea of lost hope, betrayal and eternal grief at the loss.

Father Manoel was speechless, struck by her beauty and her terrible grief. Instinctively, he raised a hand and moved to wipe away her tears.

"Don't touch her!" Martin shouted, and hurried across the studio to get between the statue and the priest.

"Oh, I'm sorry. I didn't realize. For a moment I forgot she wasn't real."

As Martin came to a stop in front of him, Father Manoel gazed at the sculptor in unveiled wonder.

"*Meu Deus*, Mr. Drake, it's the most moving thing I have ever seen. She's absolutely beautiful, but she's so, so sad. Who is she?"

"Nobody," he lied. "Just a statue."

"You made her?"

"Yes, I made her." Irony pierced him like a flaming lance. "I made her all right."

The priest looked at him, stunned and at a loss for words. His mouth moved a moment in silence, searching, then he spoke reverently to the man before him. "Could you do this for us? Could you sculpt the face of God for us? It would be a masterpiece. It would be a gift to the world."

"No. I told you to go and talk to Vicki. Now get out of here."

Martin was hot. He didn't like this man looking at his statue and into his soul.

The priest seemed not to hear him and again marveled at the bronze woman who was walking away. "Then perhaps you would let me change the contract. Let us buy this from you. Let Mr. Banks place it in a museum for all the world to see."

"She's not for sale."

"Maybe Mr. Banks would pay you more..."

"She's not for sale at any price. Now get out of here."

The priest looked at the artist with the melancholy sadness that comes the moment after one touches wonder for just a fleeting instant, knowing that he will never touch it again.

"Think it over, Mr. Drake. You have a chance to do a great thing. You can be what you pretend to be. You can be better. You are a true artist."

"Get out of here!"

Father Manoel looked for an instant into the angry eyes of the artist: they were full of life where before they had been dull and empty. He nodded, patted Martin on the shoulder and slowly walked away. Martin brushed the statue's cheek as he watched the priest leave.

Chapter Twelve

MOONLIGHT POURED INTO THE studio from the skylights above, giving life to a forest of shadows that cast themselves across the hardwood floor in a tangle of impenetrable darkness. Soft beams bathed the burnished cheek of the woman as she walked away from the sound of footsteps echoing near the edge of her nocturnal glen. Martin entered his studio, unkempt and drunk, bottle of whiskey still in hand. He muttered to himself as he walked to his work table, where he and his bottle stopped and took a seat.

"Face of God. Face of God. I could sculpt the face of God if I wanted to. I could do anything—if I wanted to. Fuck them. Fuck that priest. Fuck Armine. Fuck Vicki—now that she's pissed at me and screaming for a raise. Sue me? Eat me! Fuck her too. Who'd want to fuck her? Ha! Fuck her too. Fuck 'em all."

He took a drink then set the bottle down. He stared dully at the lump of clay before him. He tried to pick it up, but it resisted him. It was as hard and uncooperative as a rock in a scrub farmer's acre. He strained to pull it free and then pushed it to the floor, where it disappeared in shadow with a final thunk.

"Face of God...fuck them..."

He sat awhile, pondering his bottle, which stood out in the half-light where the clay had been before. He took another swig. "Face of God..."

He looked up at the moon that glimmered through the heavy paneled glass and then glanced around the room, which had been so long abandoned that it was no longer familiar at night. A big gray shape loomed beside the door, his welding machine. He rose and staggered toward it.

"I'll give them the face of God!" he cackled. With the flip of a switch the machine hummed to life. He grabbed the stinger and a small metal plate that he dropped atop the welder. Then he put on a helmet and struck an arc.

"Face of God. Happy God. Happy, happy God, God, God!" Molten lava scribed a circle on the metal plate. "Eye of God. Eye of God." Two fiery dots burst forth amid the flaming ring. "Laughing God. Smiley God. Happy, happy God, God, God." He burned an arc beneath the eyes. A happy face grinned back.

"Fuck you, smiley. Fuck you, God!" He smote the face with his lightening rod, blasting it to slag. Angry metal blew through plate and machine housing and into the screaming generator. Sparks burst forth from the heart of blue flame that threw Martin back with an angry boom.

He sat there stunned and silent for over an hour, watching the lights that played within his eyes.

Finally, he got up and walked to a cabinet, opened it and began to shuffle through its contents. He ripped open several boxes until he found two that suited him. Beneath their plastic wrappers lay two blocks of modeling clay still moist enough to work. He carried them to his table and began to shape them. The clay was stiff and unused and it fought his fingers, which were long unpracticed. He reached a hand down into the wetting bowl sunk in a recess at the table's edge, but evaporation had taken its water years earlier. *Whiskey will do*, he thought. He emptied his bottle into the lump he was kneading. It's smoky heat soon warmed the reluctant clay into a cooperative mass.

Martin's fingers molded the clay from its former shapelessness into a crude head. He concentrated as he shaped, caressed and drew with fingers, palms and thumbs, and little by little the clay became a face. It was a classical style, like a Greek or Roman bust. Hair and forehead were complete, and nose was forming when he became angry at himself and his creation. It was evolving into just another knock-off, nothing more. He frowned, and his anger returned. With the flick of a thumb, the fine nose widened. Martin worked faster. His features took a wicked turn, back to what they'd been when he was welding. He began to laugh, and his creation laughed back. His fervent, cynic fingers wove in the clay, fantastic with rapid dabs and tucks. Soon he was finished.

He cackled at the pitiful bust before him. It was Father Manoel, but it wasn't him at all. It was instead a vicious caricature of the man who plagued the sculptor, first with accusation and now with belief. It was a grinning, mindless, ugly attack.

Martin cackled on and on, then traded derision for violence. With a savage yell, he pulled the priest up by the ears and with a running heave, threw him across the room. The bust sailed high, arcing just below the towered ceiling panes. It held itself aloft for just an instant, grinning down at its creator and destroyer—looking as if it, too, had a joke to play. Then it followed its gravity-bound trajectory and struck the woman full in the face as she walked away.

"No!" screamed Martin. He raced to the statue and pulled wildly at the clay that clung to it. Tears coursed down his face, and sobs wracked his heaving chest. He smoothed away the remaining bits of clay and caressed her while choking, "No. No. No, Sharon, no," over and over again. He fell prostrate at her feet, still sobbing and mouthing silently her name. Sleep took him heavy through the night.

Chapter Thirteen

FATHER MANOEL SET HIS Bible down at the chirping of the telephone. He got up from the desk where he was reading and eased past the foot of his bed to pick up the receiver, which was mounted on the wall opposite the sink and mirror behind the door of his tiny room.

"Hello?"

"Hi, Father, this is Alph at the front desk. You got a call. Hang on a second, and I'll put it through."

Alph clicked off and was replaced by a dial tone. After several clicks he came back on the line. "Are you still there, Father?"

"Yes, Alph."

"Damn these new phones. I can't ever get it right. Hold on..."

Alph clicked off. A series of beeps spun an atonal rift, then finally a voice came on the line.

"Father Manoel?"

"Yes."

"This is Martin Drake. Where the hell are you, Father? That clown of an operator has been trying to get you for over two minutes. How hard can it be? All it takes is the push of a button."

"I'm at the Lutheran Seafarer's House at Irving Place."

"I thought you were Catholic."

"I am, very much so, but the reverend who runs this mission is an old friend of mine. How did you get my number?"

"Armine gave it to me. Look, Father, I'd like to talk to you about your sculpture."

Father Manoel squeezed the rosary he held in his hand and looked to the ceiling in a quick prayer of thanks. "Do you mean that you are going to help us, Mr. Drake?"

"We have a contract, don't we?"

Father Manoel squeezed his prayer beads harder. "That's right; we do."

"Good. Now, when can you come over to talk about it? I want to know what it is you want me to do."

"I can leave here right now, but it might take some time for me to get up to you. I'm forever taking the wrong subway train or missing my stop."

"Well, take a cab then."

"I really can't afford that."

"Oh. Well...get up here as soon as you can. I'll be expecting you. Bye." He clicked off.

Father Manoel hung up and absently kissed his rosary as he checked his watch for the time—11 a.m. Then he pushed by the bed to the small closet that held his shabby coat and gloves. As he swung open the closet door, his leg brushed into the radiator, which steamed forth shimmered heat in tropical defiance of the draft that blew through the ancient window panes above it . The warmth felt good upon his skin. He struggled into his cold weather gear, stopped and stooped to kiss his Bible, then headed out the door with yet another silent prayer of thanks.

Chapter Fourteen

MARTIN, UNWASHED AND CRUMPLED in the clothes he had been wearing the night before, coffee cup in hand, ushered the priest into his living room with a silent nod. He motioned for Father Manoel to take a seat on the sofa with a wave of his cup, then upon taking a sip, remembered basic manners.

"Do you want some coffee?"

"No thank you, my son. I had mine early in the day, but please drink yours. You look like you could use it."

Martin slumped into a Gropius armchair beside the sofa and rubbed the stubble on his chin while he regarded the priest with dry, painful eyes. His head hurt, but it would burn off eventually—quickly if he took a few wake-up pops, but then he didn't want to do that, not with the priest around. He would suffer for the moment. He took a swig of coffee, which joined the battle to clear his chronic stupor. Then he asked raspily, "Well, Father, what do you have in mind?"

"In mind?"

"Yes, what would you like me to sculpt."

"The face of God, as we agreed."

"Well, what does he look like?"

The priest regarded the sculptor for a long moment and then answered, "I really don't know. I'm not sure if he looks like anything we could comprehend."

"A burning bush maybe?"

"Ah, yes. God did appear to Moses as a burning bush. So, you've read the Old Testament, Mr. Drake?" The priest's thoughtful expression changed to slight surprise. "Forgive me if I'm startled. I didn't think that you had much interest in religion."

"Well, I suppose I haven't had much lately, but there was a time…anyway, isn't there something in the Bible about not making images to worship?"

"Yes, there is. It's the second of the Ten Commandments, Exodus 20:4: 'You shall not make for yourself a carved image.' But this refers to images created as objects of worship, as deities themselves. What you are creating would be different, an offering to God given in worship of him , not something to be worshipped in and of itself. There is a two-thousand-year-old tradition of Christian art. And besides, it was your idea to sculpt the face of God in the first place, wasn't it, Mr. Drake?"

"Yes, it was, but at the time I was operating under the influence of the profit motive and too much Scotch. You're right: I made my bed, now I'm just trying to figure out how to sleep in it. Where do you think we should go with this, then? Armine has told me that you don't like abstractions, but as far as I can see, any description of the Judeo-Christian deity is abstract. What are your ideas?"

The priest took off his ski gloves and examined his chapped fingers. He didn't have an answer. During these last five days since he had become involved with this project, he hadn't even thought about the sculpture itself—he hadn't considered that his job. He was here to find donors to support his charity, not to design sculpture. He had felt duty-bound to ensure that whatever it was that was finally delivered wouldn't be blasphemous, but that was as far as he thought his responsibility went. His ideas on what the face of God would look like? He realized that after a lifetime of service to God himself, he didn't have the slightest idea.

One didn't search for the image of God when one prayed. One didn't need to. The key to salvation was faith, and faith was blind. It was enough to know that God existed in everything, in ways beyond human comprehension. Belief and faith were the only requirements of the devout. Trying to peer through God's mystery to behold his glory was as fruitless as it was unnecessary. He would fully reveal himself in time, and that would come only at the end of this mortal life. The faithful understood this. The image of God was truly abstract, at least in human terms. He was an all-knowing, all-powerful being that dwelt in everything, in all of his creation. You could see him in the sunrise, in the dew upon the morning flowers, in the neon colors of a butterfly and in the waking moments of a newborn child, but in finite limits like those that described each individual human face? No, he was beyond such description. Trying to display all that God was, in one certain form, would be like trying to capture the sea in a teardrop, but infinitely more difficult. The most gifted visionary would fall far short. God was beyond comprehension. And which face then to sculpt? That of the Father, the Son or the Holy Ghost? Were they separate or one? Embarrassment and regret filled him. As a priest, he should have had an answer, but he didn't.

Father Manoel looked up at Martin. "I guess I don't know what God looks like. No living person could. Traditional Christian art is full of saints, angels, the Madonna, and Jesus Christ as both man and child, and there are various depictions of God the Father hidden in a cloud with rays of his light beaming from it. He has also been personified as a wise and aged but powerful man, like Michelangelo painted him on the ceiling of the Sistine Chapel. But you are right. These are images meant to reduce God to something understandable to us. Christ was a man, but the picture that we have of him today is based on nothing more than conjecture—what a man living in Judea in that time would most probably have looked like. He is most often viewed as handsome, but who can say if he was? There are those who think he might have been Black . In fact, there are altar Christs in some colonial Brazilian churches that are Black. These were churches built by slaves, and maybe they were right. Maybe Christ was Black. It's not important. Is it?"

"No, I suppose not," answered Martin. He took another sip of coffee. "But if his image isn't important, then why don't you just go with one of Vicki's sketches?"

"Now wait a minute, Mr. Drake." Father Manoel straightened in his seat, and his voice rose in agitation. "The tradition in Christian art is to venerate God, to represent him as beautiful and wise and loving, to show him and the world how dear he is to us. I don't think that even your esoteric clients would appreciate her work on this. There is a fine line between what is shocking and what is offensive, and she would surely cross it. Though I personally think she crossed it long ago."

Martin motioned for calm with a sweep of his cup.

"No, Father, I'm not suggesting that we turn to Vicki for this one—besides you won't let me. No, I'll do the work, but we need to know where to start. God has always been an enigma, and for some of us he still is."

Martin smiled, then continued. "Man has been attempting art for at least 15,000 years. The first known

106

drawings were painted in caves in southern France and northern Spain during the last Ice Age, pictures of bison and horses. It is believed that they were drawn to aid in the hunt, as if the cavemen thought that by capturing the image of an animal, it would somehow magically help them grab the animal itself. Later, as man evolved, he created images of his gods, again thinking that a carved or painted representation could somehow intercede on his behalf—if it was evoked through religious rituals and prayers. These totems often took the form of known animals such as jaguars, wolves or crocodiles, or of fanciful beasts like the Aztec feathered serpent god, Quetzalcoatl. Fertility or harvest goddesses were often depicted as gravid women or animals.

"As civilizations advanced, gods were given more human characteristics. Most of the Egyptian gods had bodies of men but heads of animals, such as the jackal-headed Anubis or the hawk-headed Horus. With the coming of the Greeks, gods were given human form. The Greeks, and later the Romans, sculpted their gods with ideal proportions and features that reflected their type of deity. Zeus, king of the gods, was stern and majestic and was often shown delivering his wrath to straying subjects with a javelin throw of his mighty thunderbolt. Apollo, god of light, truth and poetry, was lean and strong and more handsome than the rising sun, while Aphrodite, goddess of love, was beyond beautiful with her plump, round lines of perfect grace and loveliness.

"After the fall of Rome, Western religious art dwelt mainly with the passion of Christ, and the persecution of the saints—statues, triptychs, reliquaries, paintings and lots and lots of Christs on a stick. But you don't want a crucified Jesus with a crown of thorns and forlorn tears, do you?"

"I really don't know, Mr. Drake. Perhaps if you do it beautifully like you sculpted that woman..."

"No thanks, Father. I don't see a whole lot of difference between your stricken Jesuses and my tortured mannequins."

Father Manoel started with the realization of the similarity between the two. He looked to the sculptor, mind gearing for argument, and said, "But that's not fair! The crucifixion is a symbol of the love of God for mankind, a symbol of our inherent sin and Christ's sacrifice for us and covenant with us, which cleanses us and makes us worthy to stand before our Father. Your mannequins are just a mockery of this."

"Variations on a theme, Father, but I don't want to get into that. No, if I'm going to do this, I'd like to do something other than Christ. We'll skip him, he's been done. We'll concentrate on the Godhead, the Trinity—the Father, Son and Holy Ghost. Let's try to do something memorable."

Martin looked down to his cup and saw that it was empty.

"Excuse me, I need more coffee. Are you sure you don't want some?"

"Thank you, my son, perhaps I would."

They got up, and Father Manoel followed Martin to the kitchen. Martin poured two cups of coffee, handed one to Father Manoel and then pointed to the sugar jar on the shelf above the counter. Father Manoel pulled it down and added two spoonfuls to his coffee. Martin started to reach for the whiskey bottle sitting on the countertop but caught himself and stopped. Instead, he topped off his cup with hot coffee and sipped it, his fourth cup that morning. The caffeine buzzed up to his clearing head. He looked to the priest and asked, "Now, where were we?"

"You said you didn't want to do a crucified Christ."

"Yeah, he's been pretty well covered, so let's get back to...what was it?"

"Medieval art."

"Oh yes, medieval art. Gothic art. Gothic art was a big step backward. The fluidity of movement of Greek statuary, thickened in the hands of the Romans and then turned to stone at the fall of the Empire. Sculpture was lifeless for the better part of a millennium. Let's skip it and move on to the Renaissance. Now the Renaissance brought the revival of classical themes in sculpture and the improvement of their execution. It was an age of superb sculptors that the world has yet to see again. It began I think, though others might disagree, with Donatello in Florence around the beginning of the fifteenth century. He put life and grace back into sculpture. His bronze of the young David showed a fineness and a sense of movement that the world hadn't seen since the Golden Age of Greece, and maybe not even then. He was followed by all the great masters: Cellini, Goujon, Leonardo da Vinci, Giovanni da Bologna, Michelangelo— you mentioned his work on the Sistine Chapel. You can't imagine the speed with which he painted it. Alone, on his back, lying precariously atop a wooden scaffold, he painted the vastness of that ceiling in all its complexity of figures and color in just four years. He worked as quickly as he could because he felt that it was keeping him from his true calling—sculpture. He didn't want to take the job in the first place and felt as if he was forced into it. But he had to take it: you couldn't say no to the Pope in those days."

"Some of us still can't," interjected the priest.

Martin smiled. "No, I suppose not.

"That was an age, Father. There has never been such a concentration of talented sculptors in the world since, and I doubt there ever will be."

Martin looked down to his cup and saw that it was empty again.

"Would you like some more, Father?"

"No thank you. My cup is still full."

Martin refilled his cup and said, "Let's go back into the living room."

In the living room, he led Father Manoel to a large bookcase, set his coffee down on an end table and began looking at titles. As he found those he wanted, he pulled them from the shelf and set them next to his coffee.

"Look, Father, here are some books on art. This one's on modern American sculpture."

He handed it to Father Manoel.

"Why don't you take it home and thumb through it. It might give you some ideas. Hell, take them all. And do me a favor. Spend today and tomorrow in the museums around here: the Metropolitan, the MOMA, the Guggenheim, the Whitney's good..."

"Here's what we'll do. Why don't you do a little reading first to get an idea of what you're looking at and then go to the museums. I'll call Armine and have her call the curators to let them know you're coming, so they'll give you a private tour. Then come back here...what day is today?"

"Thursday."

"Okay. Come back here Monday around, let's say, one in the afternoon, and I'll have some solid ideas to go over with you then."

"Mr. Drake?"

"Call me Martin. What is it?"

"Martin," the priest said. "Why the change of heart? You threw me out of here yesterday, and now you're going out of your way to be helpful. What happened to make you want to change your mind?"

Martin rubbed the stubble on his chin as though searching for an answer. Father Manoel watched him. As grubby as Martin was, he seemed more alive than when they'd met that night in the gallery amidst the flashing cameras and clapping crowds. Martin had seemed listless then. But now, even though he looked as if he had drained a bottle and slept in the street, Martin looked alive. His eyes, though puffy and red, were animated. Father Manoel was shocked at the change as much as he'd been shocked by his sense of wonder at the statue of the woman.

Martin looked to the priest, then answered, "Oh, I don't know, Father. I guess you could say that last night I saw an old friend whom I haven't seen in a long, long time and that friend gave me a little kick in the butt. Now look at these books…"

He shuffled through them and read off the names scrolled on their spines, "We've got Rodin, Calder, Giacometti, Henry Moore—here's one on Dyak tribal art."

Martin thumbed through the thick tome and then picked up another one. "What do you know about free-form abstraction?"

Father Manoel answered with a blank look.

"Well, this might take a while. Grab half of these and let's sit down at the dinner table over there."

They struggled their stacks to the table.

"Let's start with Rodin," said Martin. "He was magnificent. He did one in marble called the 'Hand of God' that shows Adam and Eve forming from the firmament held in God's hand. It's outstanding. Now if I could do something like that…set those books down and have a seat. Here's the book on Rodin. Let's see if we can find it…"

Chapter Fifteen

"COME IN," SAID MARTIN. He stepped back to allow the priest passage into his living room. Father Manoel lurched in with the heavy sack of books he was carrying and stopped to balance it on the back of a chair. Martin closed and bolted the door, then said, "Let's go into the studio."

"Would you like me to put these back on your bookshelf first?"

"No, bring them with you; maybe they'll inspire me."

They walked through the living room and into the studio, Martin striding ahead unencumbered, followed by the priest who was still lugging the heavy sack. As they entered the studio, Martin pointed and said, "Put them over there with the rest."

There were two large stacks of books staggering up the nearest wall in crooked, risky helixes , and they were cornered by a company of other books, flipped open in a random jumble scattered around the parquet floor. The work table was another mess. It was heaped with paper and cups, an empty whiskey bottle and great gobs of slick and formless clay. The remains of a ravaged pizza littered the table's edge above a ream of crumpled paper, and on the floor across the room was a battalion of heads, some wizened and regal, some enlightened and others looking down in abysmal sadness—all were starkly sublime. It was as if the Grim Reaper had ridden through at night, claiming all his markers on the best and most noble the universe could provide, in one fell swoop.

Father Manoel maneuvered through the clutter and knelt before the kings. He offered his fealty to each in turn. "Martin, these are all outstanding. They are magnificent!"

The sculptor, pacing beyond the table, ignored the praise and asked, "Did you visit the museums over the weekend like I asked you to?"

Father Manoel answered, "Yes I did," not lifting his eyes from the busts he was admiring. His pleasure in them was obvious.

"Well, what did you see that inspired you? What ideas have you brought me?"

Father Manoel, who still studied the busts, replied, "I saw many marvelous things in the museums—art like I've never seen before in my entire life. I couldn't begin to tell you...I wouldn't know where to start, but nothing I saw is any better than these, Martin. These are just like some of the statues in the museums. They are just as good. Maybe better."

He looked up to see the sculptor frowning down on him.

"Just like what you saw at the museums. Just as good. Maybe better. So what you're telling me is that what you're looking at is no different than what you saw in the museums?"

Father Manoel gazed confusedly at the agitated man above him, and answered, "There were many, many wonderful sculptures in the museums, many different types of things. Some were gorgeous. Some I couldn't appreciate, but these, these are like the sculptures of God, which I liked best."

"Just like what you saw. Just like what you saw." The sculptor started pacing again.

"What's the matter, Martin? I don't understand why you're upset. You've done it. You've done what we asked you to do. You've succeeded. Anyone of these busts would be wonderful. You pick the one you want to do for me. They are all so good that I don't want to choose between them. I wish I could have them all, but I know that we only have a contract for one."

Martin paced back toward the priest, glowering as he went. "Don't you know anything? Are you stupid?"

The priest, through a welter of confusion, watched Martin pacing, and stood.

"What's the matter, my son? Why are you angry? You should be proud."

"Proud of what? Of my ability to mimic? You hate Vicki, but at least she's original. You want me to be proud of my knack at copying? Wow! Oh boy, Martin Drake, supreme knock-off artist. That's just what I want to be! Look at these." He bent down and lifted one up.

"Ever see this guy before?"

"Of course, that's Jesus."

"That's right! You got it, Father. Good old Jesus. Old sweet Jesus. The same one that's tacked up in every barn of a Catholic church across the country. A monkey could do this. Where's the art?"

"But it's beautiful, Martin."

"Beautiful as any you could buy from a discount church supplier. This is junk." Martin brought the bust down hard into the largest glob of clay on his table. With a loud *thwop*, Jesus melded with the muck.

"Please, Martin. No. Why did you do that? He was beautiful." He put a hand on Martin's arm, but the sculptor pulled away.

"Goddamn it, Father. I thought you wanted something special. You wanted Baccarat crystal when I met you. Now you're into Dixie cups. Fine! Fine! Just step right up, then. Pick one out, and I'll run him off the line in a jiffy, customarily clean and smiling bright."

The priest saw the frustration that fumed forth from Martin's boiling eyes.

"I think I understand, my son. You're upset because what you've done here isn't original. I can understand that you, as an artist, want to be unique, but Martin think about it—you're following in the footsteps of a two-thousand-year-old tradition. Generations upon generations of sculptors have sought to achieve what you've done several times over in a single weekend. Of course your busts resemble those of the past. How could they not? That doesn't matter. They are beautiful in their own right."

"Damn it, Father. Don't you understand? Anybody can make those things."

"I can't."

"Well, anyone who calls himself an artist. You say they're beautiful. Big deal! Big-breasted, fine-featured, leggy blondes are beautiful too, and they all flock to Hollywood to be in pictures, swaying and jiggling, all hoping to be a star. And how many of them make it? One in a thousand? One in ten thousand? And what makes the lucky one different from the rest? What is it she has that hexes the celluloid and flashes her forth bigger than life across the world for the mindless masses to drool over? All the pretty little starlets look good in the sack, but what makes the chosen one different?"

Father Manoel stood silent, wondering from where this passion flooding Martin had burst. He answered, "I don't know."

"Well, I don't know either, but these guys don't have it."

He kicked the busts over, one by one.

Father Manoel walked away, not wanting to witness the scene. He had never met anyone who was capable of creating what Martin had created, and he had never seen anyone react with such violent disgust against their own work... except himself when he was carried out of the Amazon . He shivered and walked away toward the scatter of books.

Martin raved at him from the worktable where he was taking the heads of the fallen gods and mashing them back into the growing globs atop the table.

"Do you know how many beautiful women I've slept with, Father?"

The priest didn't answer. He wasn't listening.

"I don't either, but probably hundreds, all dying to taste the salt of the artist, all wanting to be touched by the hand of creation. And do you know how many women I've ever been in love with? One. One girl in my whole life, and she left me because she couldn't stand me anymore. One out of hundreds. And what made her different from all of the rest?

"I don't know myself. I honestly don't know. She had everything; the rest, nothing. She had what it took to take my breath away, to capture my imagination, and she took it and left. The rest are clay, just like these busts."

Father Manoel was lost. It was as if, over the weekend, this hopeless sot he had been chained to had somehow become a righteous, raving fiend. He was having trouble adjusting, and he was alarmed. From experience he knew that the price of failure for the zealot possessed could be very high indeed. He wanted to calm the artist, but didn't know what to say.

He looked at the pictures casting themselves up from the pages of the open books on the floor. Most resembled the busts that Martin had just destroyed. In the middle of them all was an ancient book flipped open to reveal a spray of solar color. He stepped over to get a closer look. It was a majestic, windblown man kneeling down from his place in the sun, scribing the bounds of the universe with a golden compass in the blackness that surrounded his light. He bent down to pick up the book.

"Hey! Be careful with that!" Martin stormed over, took the book away and cradled it tenderly in his hands as if it were a favorite son. "This is an original. There are only twelve left in the world."

Father Manoel was slightly miffed at the agitated sculptor. "I wasn't going to hurt it. I just thought it was striking."

"I'm sorry, but it's special to me. The man who printed this could have given you want you need. He was a true original, just like his book." Martin gently handed it back to the priest.

"Who is he?"

"William Blake. This is *Europe: A Prophesy*. That same picture you're looking at hangs in the British Museum. It's God scribing the universe from Milton's *Paradise Lost*."

"It's gorgeous."

"Yeah, it is, isn't it? And Blake didn't consider himself primarily an artist. He used engravings to illustrate his poetry. He invented a color printing process and painstakingly engraved his 'illuminated poems' himself, because he didn't want anybody to come between him and his work. He was born relatively poor but managed to get into the Royal Academy. He broke from the traditional artists, though, early in life, and went his own way. He was a rebel. He saw angels. And he traded a chance at success for poverty in order to write the poems he thought the world should hear, all illustrated as he thought they should be.

117

And later, when he lay on his deathbed in obscure penury, he laughed and was happy, a fulfilled man. He lived his life, and he wouldn't be dictated to by mindless art critics or any yahoo like you. Would he have accepted a commission like this one, where I work under the whims of a priest? Ha!"

Martin rubbed his chin for a moment while he dredged the verses from his muddied memory. Then he quoted:

I went to the Garden of Love,
And saw what I never had seen:
A Chapel was built in the midst,
Where I used to play on the green.
And the gates of this Chapel were shut,
And 'thou shalt not' writ over the door;
So I turn'd to the Garden of Love
That so many sweet flowers bore;

And I saw it was filled with graves,
And tomb-stones where flowers should be;
And Priests in black gowns were walking their rounds,
And binding with briars my joys & desires.

Father Manoel looked up from the book and chuckled. Martin went on, "So he died poor and obscure, considered a lunatic, while I'm rich and famous and considered a genius. And he's now hung in the British Museum, and his poetry is considered some of the most original and important ever written in English. Will anyone remember me for what I've done? Why bother? I give the public what it wants: service with a smile, just like Burger King—have it your way! Have it your way!..." He ended the song with a scowl. "No, if there is anything behind this face of God you want me to sculpt, old Bill Blake is up in heaven, still laughing and still seeing his angels. I hope he is, anyway."

Father Manoel carefully returned Martin's book. The sculptor walked over and set it down atop a sketchpad on the worktable. The priest followed him and glanced down at a sketch lying next to the book: it intrigued him. He picked it up and studied it. It was a transparent representation of the Trinity. The face of the Son, transposed over that of the Father, delicately done as if the two were one. Enveloping their splendor was an eerie blue glow that surely represented the Holy Spirit.

"This is very interesting Martin."

"Think so? Like it?"

"Yes, very much! It's powerful. And you can't tell me that you copied it from someone else. I don't believe it."

"Nope, Father, that's an original Martin Drake all right. Now just answer me one thing."

"Sure."

"How the fuck am I gonna sculpt it?"

Father Manoel saw the problem, squeezed his stymied lips together and sighed. "I see what you mean."

"I know some people that work in glass, and I've seen some jewels that are bored and carved from the inside like a reversed intaglio. I've thought about trying to carve it out of quartz—Jesus on the outside, God on the inside, and maybe we could use fiberoptic lighting to bring out the Ghost, but I've never worked in quartz. It would take me a year to learn how to do something like this, and anyway, if I did it in quartz, it would have to be small—I don't think crystals grow ten feet high. Transparent plastic, maybe? Plexiglass? I don't think so. There are enough plastic Jesuses stuck on pious dashboards. I don't want to be the one who makes the granddaddy of them all. I thought about blown glass, but you can't work glass like this. I can't do it, and if it can be done, you'd better get somebody else, not me."

Martin started pacing again, back and forth, back and forth, until he came to a stop in front of a window on which he rested his forehead. His foot began to tap, and he started rapping angrily on the icy windowpane. Rap, rap, rap, rap. Tap, tap, tap, tap.

Father Manoel poured over the sketch, trying to think of a way to help the artist, even though he knew absolutely nothing about art, as if his unfocused concentration might in some way lead to a breakthrough. He absently walked the sketch over to the end of the studio where the statue of the woman walked away. He looked to her, her bronze locks, her resigned lips locked in their eternal quiver, her timeless tears of hopeless, broken-hearted sadness. *How lovely you are,* he thought, *so lovely, so sad.*

Martin's outrage boomed behind him, "Oh, great. Look at that—the two conspirators whispering in the corner. How sweet! What hoops are we going to make Martin jump through now? Go on! Walk away, Sharon. You already did, remember? Go on. Disappear.

"Why don't you go too, Father. You're not doing a Goddamn bit of good here. Go on. Give me a call in a few days, maybe I'll have come up with something by then."

Father Manoel walked back to the table and started to set the sketch down on top of the Blake book.

"Take that with you. It's a freebie. A Drake original. Sell it for cab fare so you don't have to take the subway all the time. I don't want to see it anymore."

"Thank you, Martin. I'll frame it and hang it in our parish church. It's wonderful."

"Whatever. Just go now, Father. I need to be alone. Call me in a week. I'll work on this. Don't worry. You'll get your statue."

"I'll pray for you, my son."

"Oh good! That ought to really help. Why don't you pray me up another pizza too. I'm starting to get hungry. Call me in a week."

"Shouldn't you walk me to the door, so you can lock it behind me?"

"Fuck the door. There's nothing here worth stealing."

Father Manoel took the drawing and left.

Martin watched him go, then turned to watch Sharon walk away.

"Go on."

He thumped his head on the pane of frozen glass.

Chapter Sixteen

THAT'S IT. YES. MAYBE. Something like this might just work. Martin painstakingly placed the thin clay squares upon the wire frame. He was carefully placing clay to cover the gap along the ridge above the left eye when the chin gave way and slid free, plopping onto the table in a formless, earthy glob. *Damn. Oh well, I'll fix that in a minute.* He smoothed out the square on the forehead until it suited him and then carefully picked up another square from where he had shaped it on the wax paper. This square he laid out parallel to the one he had just set, concealing another small block of chicken-wire mesh. He meticulously smoothed and watered the clay to bring in the edges so they aligned perfectly with the hairline above it and with the patch to its left. The seam was barely but surely evident. *That's it....*

His concentration was broken by the chirp of an electronic canary. He continued to smooth the patch, but the canary chirped away with mindless, determined gusto. Martin hesitated, then reluctantly eased his fingers from the clay and got up to answer the cordless phone singing from its perch atop his burned-out welder. He smudged its shiny surface as he grabbed it with his soiled, sweaty hand.

"Hello."

"Good morning, Martin. Rise and shine."

"I'm working, Armine."

"My, that is a surprise," she said in an iron, sarcastic clank.

"I'm working on the Banks' commission."

"Good for you, Martin. You're up, awake and working before noon. I wish I knew how to show you my genuine and heartfelt appreciation."

"What's wrong, Armine? You were bitching at me for a week to get started on this, and now I'm working on it. What else do you want?"

"Just a few little things, like showing up at your studio once in a while to keep your people from quitting..."

"Those guys quit?"

"Oh no, not all of them dear: only four out of six, just the four that had been there the longest—you know, the ones with experience. Give the other two another week to get fed up working for the invisible man and Quasimoda, the girl hunchback. Did you even know their names?"

He tried to pull them up, but only drew a blank. He answered with silence.

"No, I didn't think you would. Weren't you supposed to talk to those guys the beginning of last week?"

"Yeah, I was, Armine. Vicki mentioned that again to me yesterday, but I forgot. I was busy working on this. I should have gone. Vicki didn't say that they quit, though. I'm sorry."

"You should be. Yes, they got in a row with Vicki yesterday afternoon when they knocked off, and only two showed up for work this morning. And to make it worse, Vicki and I had it out this morning too—that priest told her how much the Banks' job is worth, so she's screaming for a raise. She told me that you told her to talk to me about it. I told her she was crazy."

Martin sighed. Another thing he'd forgotten.

"I did tell Vicki to talk to you about a raise," he said. "You're the one who cuts her checks. She called over here bitching the day before I started this thing. She wanted a one hundred percent pay hike and was threatening to quit and to sue. I explained to her how this Banks' job was a charity deal, and that's how come the price is so inflated. I'm the one who's doing it, anyway. And I told her that we'd give her something substantial, but that I'd have to discuss it with you first."

"We're not giving her anything, Martin," hissed Armine. "You are. My commission's on a gross, not a cost, basis. And my accounting fee is hourly. Whatever she gets comes out of your pocket, but you'd better make it sweet because she was foaming at the mouth when she left here. Get a hold of her fast and make her happy. We can't afford to lose her now, especially so shorthanded. Promise me you'll take care of this, Martin. Promise me! They were already behind at the factory before those guys quit, and without Vicki there to pull us through, we are going to start losing money soon. Promise me?"

"Okay, Armine. I'll talk to Vicki."

"Today, Martin. Hours and days count to everybody else but you. When I hang up, you call around and find her."

"All right. I'll do it. I said I would."

"Good. Now, how's your project coming? Is the Black priest giving you too hard a time?"

"Well, we haven't quite got it worked out yet."

"Just give him a Jesus for Christ's sake, like the gold ones they wear around their necks or like those velvet ones they sell by the interstate on the way to Miami."

"That's Mexican stuff, Armine. This guy's Brazilian."

"Whatever. Just find out what he wants and give it to him. Let's get this thing done."

"I'm trying, Armine."

"Well stop trying and do it. If that bastard's really riding you, maybe I can sweet-talk Banks into reeling him in a little. I tried flirting with Paco to move things along, but it fell flat. He probably likes boys."

"Come on, Armine. He's a priest."

"Well, what do you think men become priests for, Martin? Free bread and wine?"

"I'll talk to you later, Armine. I've got work to do."

"Get a hold of Vicki and straighten her out."

"I will. Bye."

He clicked the phone to standby, looked at it a moment, then switched the ringer off. The answering machine could pick up any messages. He'd talk to Vicki later, but right now he had to work out this idea while it was still hot on his mind.

He set the phone down and turned toward his worktable just in time to witness the mud slide. It started at the sculpture's hairline where the roots were too thin to hold up the mass of vertical, saturated grade. The clay moved slowly, forehead sliding first. Then it gathered momentum as the bridge of the nose pulled free. In an instant, all above the cheek bones was a killing force destroying all that stood in its path below. Martin ran and lunged in an attempt to save the neck and jaw, but he only managed to knock free the sticky pate, which flew forth in expanding strings until it finally struck the floor where it splayed out like a road-killed tarantula.

"Fuck! Fuck! Fuck!" he shouted.

He cocked an arm to backhand the frame but stopped himself mid-stroke. His anger would only cost him added labor. He fumed awhile at the chicken-wire head, and then, resigned to the loss of his morning's effort, walked to the kitchen and poured himself a drink.

Martin sat there and drank, glad to be away from the disaster, wondering if the idea he had was workable. It didn't seem so at the moment, but if Armine hadn't had interrupted him, he would have caught the damage in time to save it. Now he would have to start all over. He drained his whiskey and then poured himself another. *Yes, there was nothing to do but start over.* He brought his glass up to his lips but didn't take a drink. *No,* he thought, *better not. This is hard enough as it is.* He put the tumbler on the counter, took a deep breath and returned to the studio.

The chicken-wire phantom hovered over the inert mound of clay that he had tried but failed to mold to life. The spirit was strong. The flesh, not so much. *Well, one more time.*

Martin moved to his worktable, gathered up the clay into three large lumps and began to roll them out, one by one, as if he were a baker preparing for the holidays. He had once had a kitchen rolling pin for this kind of work, but like many other things, it had abandoned him and disappeared. He used an empty bottle now instead. As he bore down upon the clay, he could feel the muscles in his back strain like wires beneath his skin. It felt animalistic and good. The slick clay felt good beneath his fingers, and its musty scent took him off to a nature that he had never visited. The work moved quickly, and soon he was cutting out the squares and odd shapes with which he hoped to transform the chicken wire into God. He didn't cut to template or to measure. He cut by eye, instinctively and exact, and when he had finished the cutting, he went over and lifted up the clay tarantula from the floor, as if he thought he could bring it back to life. He set it on his bench and shaped it roughly with rolling palms and probing fingers. Then he set it atop the barren, waiting wire. In an instant, the form had hair. He wet his hands and picked up a clay square, which would soon become a cheek. The real work had begun.

Martin eased the clay onto the frame, deftly forcing it to properly contour, but not allowing it to press through the wire and reveal the pattern beneath it. Carefully and tirelessly, he fitted the pieces one by one into the forming puzzle. He worked, not from memory, but from vision— and never erred in placement. As he worked on the nose, the still-soft clay of an ear stretched loose and readied for a dive. He caught it and smoothed it home, then returned to the nose that, neglected by him, had begun to answer instead to the siren call of gravity. He caught it too, and his fingers reasoned it back into place. In three short hours, he was back to where he had been before, bringing forth a forehead from the loam. Then the silence of his crucible was shattered by a loud and intent drumming on his apartment door.

Shit. He held the square up with his right hand and dipped his left in water. Carefully, with watered fingertips, he eased it in place above the gap that would become a brow. The pounding went on unabated, and Vicki's voice began to shrill above it. *Shit. Hold on, just a second.* He smoothed the clay with a final sweep of his thumbs, then ran to answer the door.

He threw back the locks and flung the door open.

"Hi, Vick. Come in."

"Martin, I've had about enough of you and that dumb cunt Armine!" she shouted.

"I know, I heard. Come on in."

As she walked past him, he slammed the door behind her, flipping a bolt into place.

"Let's go to the studio." He ran back to his work. She followed.

The square above the missing eyebrow had chosen independence and was pulling itself free when he caught it and pressed it back in place. He was calming the other rioters when Vicki laid into him.

"Goddamn you, Martin, you promised me a raise! I went to see that bitch like you told me to, and all she did was smile and play dumb. Who's fucking me here, Martin? You or her? Where's my raise?"

"Calm down, Vicki. Calm down," he said, as he tried to both prop up a peeling cheek and look over his shoulder to talk.

"I don't want to calm down! I want to get paid what I'm worth. How much have you been screwing me for all these years, Martin?" She glared at him. Tears ran from her puffy eyes and down her round and downy cheeks.

"If you're getting a million for that mud man you're making, how much have you been getting for my pretty mannequins? I do all the work, you bastard, and do I live on Park Avenue? Do I have a nice home studio where I can loll around all day taking it easy, tinkering, while all the dumbfucks down at the factory bust their asses to make me rich? No. What have I got? A two-bedroom walk-up in Jersey City with banging pipes and niggers for neighbors. Have any drive-by shootings in this part of town? Well, if you want some, just move across the river.

"You've been using me, Martin. I put my heart into everything I've ever done for you, and what do I get in return? I get shit on and robbed. You've been using me all along, and I thought you were my friend..." Tears poured forth in big snorty sobs. She walked away and leaned upon his welder, choking and cursing angry sorrow at the wall.

Martin was moved and stood up to comfort her. He thought she was warped, a casualty of some awful trauma of which he never knew or thought to ask, but he did, in his way, care for her. She was the one honest person he knew, other than the priest, and even though he often drew her along and toyed with her, he did respect her hard work and dedication. Not her dedication to him—that was foolish—but her dedication to her art, however strange it might be. He felt guilty, now that he had been caught, for using her. He didn't want to see her cry. A happy, self-possessed Vicki had always been a distraction that made him laugh. Neither of them was laughing now.

He walked to her and put his arm around her.

"Get off me, you asshole." She pushed him away and hugged herself into her coat. He tried again.

"I said, get off of me!"

She moved to the windows facing the park far below. Then she turned to face him.

"Look," she sobbed. "I want a pay increase, at least double what I'm getting, and I want a percentage from now on. That dumb cunt gets twelve percent, doesn't she? Well, maybe I should get fifteen."

Greed clicked on. Guilt clicked off.

"I can't give you fifteen percent, Vicki," he said. "Don't be ridiculous."

"Why not. It's my ideas and my work. Why the fuck shouldn't I get fifteen percent?"

"I can't afford that!"

"Well, you'd better start economizing. Move in with one of those rich bitches you're pounding and put this place on the market. Rent's cheap in Jersey City—well, not cheap for me, but a hot shot like you can afford a big place there."

"Vicki, now let's be reasonable. I agree, you deserve more, and I'll give you more. But you're not getting a percentage."

"Well, then you can find yourself another fool, Martin. I've had enough."

He was getting angry. Every time he started making progress on his sculpture, somebody interrupted him, and he was tired of it. He wanted to help her out—she deserved more money, but he wasn't going to be dictated to. He'd give her something, and eventually she'd settle down and forget about it. He knew her weaknesses. He would use them.

"Where are you going to go?" he asked.

"I don't know, but I'll find a job with someone who won't screw me every time I walk through the door. I bet I could get a job with any sculptor in town, doing studio work. They'll cream over my new designs, and those mannequins will sell as good for anybody else as they do for you, asshole."

His heating blood cooled to ice. He was running out of patience. "Now listen to me, Vick. For one thing, any design coming out of my studio, including the mannequins and the drawings you've been working on, is mine. Remember the contract you signed?"

Her tear-swollen face flushed red with anger.

"That's my work, Martin!"

"Wrong, Vicki. It's mine, and another thing, I doubt very much that you'd get a job with anybody else after I put the word out on you."

She glared hatred through her tears.

"You bastard. You motherfucker!"

She swung to hit him, but he caught her hand and gripped it firm. She struggled to break free.

"Let me loose. You're hurting me!"

He let it go, and she pulled it away, massaging it.

"Well, I don't need to work for anybody else. I could start sculpting under my own name."

"And who's going to buy from you, Vick? Do you think anybody's going to want a Martin Drake knock-off copped from a disgruntled studio hand, when they can get the original from me? And besides, half of this business is salesmanship and showmanship, and I don't think that either is your strong suit."

She looked away and then glanced down at her chubby hands, which were wringing themselves a hiding place in the bulge of her soft belly. She knew he was right. She could never make it on her own. She might if he helped her, but she could see that he wouldn't. All those years of dedicated work had gotten her nothing. And all of those years of friendship? Nothing but lies. They had used her all along, and they weren't about to stop now. Her resolve died. She was defeated.

He put a firm had on her shoulder. She shrugged weakly, but let it stay. He had planned to double her pay when she walked through the door, but now he was angry at her, at Armine and at interruptions in general. Magnanimity had flown.

"Look, Vick, you are valuable to me, and I appreciate you and your work very much. But don't take advantage of my goodwill. I'll give you a twenty-five percent pay hike on base and fifteen percent on overtime. That's generous, and you know it."

She didn't.

"And you'll get a two-thousand-dollar bonus if you can meet our fulfillment schedules even though those other guys quit. I'll try to get somebody else as soon as I can, but in the meantime, get back down to the factory and get back to work."

She looked at the floor and nodded. Eyes that had always been direct and full of light, were now averted and clouded with resentment. As she turned to walk out, she glanced across the room to the workbench, where she saw ammunition for a parting shot.

"Hey boss, looks like your mud man needs a face lift."

Then she walked out and was gone.

Martin spun to see the chicken-wire phoenix rise featherless from the brown and sticky clay. It had fallen to pieces again.

"Fuck!"

He stormed over and punched it to the floor, stoving-in twelve hours of labor and scraping his knuckles in the process.

"Fuck!"

He needed a drink.

Chapter Seventeen

WHEN MARTIN STEPPED INTO his studio, it was as if he stepped into a war zone—downtown Sarajevo, Kigali, East LA after the riots, someplace, anyplace—littered with the refuse of man's senseless slaughter. Sketches were strewn like debris shelled out of buildings, and scattered amid the wreck and rubble were the hapless attempts of last night's failure, the disembodied casualties of the battle he was losing. It was a wasteland.

As he moved through his mess, Martin's depression grew. He sat down at his bench and surveyed the dismal scene, wondering when and if inspiration would come. His head hurt, as always, but the hangover didn't matter. It was the dull thud of failure banging up from his gut that made him want to disappear.

During the last week, he had burned for something for the first time in a decade. He had tried to bring an idea to life, to shape it and make it concrete, and now he felt burned out. He'd searched for vision but felt surely blind. The one idea that held promise had flopped back into the primal ooze from which he had tried to pull it. If there was a God, he knew the world would be a vacuum.

Maybe he'd just give the priest any old bust and be done with it. The priest would be satisfied, and his satisfaction was inked in the contract, not Martin's.

Martin wasn't even sure what satisfaction was. It was to him what sex was to a eunuch, just a strange and empty concept that made him feel slightly uncomfortable and embarrassed. Maybe it was time to give up again and slip back into the familiar role of Martin Drake, pop artist and socialite. The role was calling him with the dreamy whispers of a warm bed on a cold, snowy morning.

He glanced around the room and sighed. Time to throw in the towel. Then his eyes caught the eyes of bronze that still shed tears of accusing sadness, as she turned and walked away.

"I tried," he spoke aloud, annoyed. "Why did you expect so much, anyway? Can't you see I can't do this?"

Martin swallowed and turned away. There, on the floor, was the framework of the bust that had twice self-destructed the day before. He rubbed his bruised knuckles as he pondered it. It was the one idea that had been both workable and good. But it hadn't been workable after all, just more stardust, a carrot held before a hungry mule. It was as useless and as dangerous as Icarus' wings, tantalizing but suicidal. Men really weren't meant to fly; they were meant to slog through the muck. And he wasn't meant to sculpt in clay; he was meant to wallow in it. He felt like crying.

Looking away from the battered armature of yet another failed attempt, Martin stared out the window, the one farthest from Sharon. He didn't need to see her now. The sun was up and shining through the glass, which was traced with icy, cobwebbed finery.

Martin walked to the window, leaned his head against its cold surface and stared glumly at the ledge outside. It was crusted with pigeon shit and snow, and a rusty hank of old window screen that had somehow managed to hang on over the years. The screens had been removed before he bought the place, so he was surprised to see a remnant there.

He looked at the fine rows of rusty checkers and thought it strange that it had managed to hold its ground all this time, not at all like those thin squares of clay that had failed him. Wait a minute...*That was it!*

Martin pulled the latch and struggled to push open the window. With a snap of broken ice, it lifted. He reached out and grabbed the orphaned bit of screen and took it to his workbench, where he rolled out another of his thin clay crusts. He pressed the screen into the clay and folded more clay over it, sandwiching it in. Then with an Exacto knife, he cut the clay, first in strips and then in squares. He picked one up and plied it back and forth. *Perfect.* The clay-and-screen sandwich held whatever shape he bent. *This is going to work,* he thought. The armature was soon back on the table, wired with a wreath of clay patches. *It's going to work!*

Almost at a gallop, Martin blew into his living room and toppled a pile of magazines to get at the phone book. He thumbed through the Yellow Pages until he found a hardware store near him—there weren't many near the Upper West Side. The phone beeped a rift as he punched in the numbers. It rang several times.

"Klotsky Hardware. Hold please."

Nothing for a solid minute.

"Klotsky Hardware. Can I help you?"

"Hi, do you sell screen?"

"What kind of screen?"

"Metal screen, like window screen?"

"Kind of late in the year. You got a snow fly problem?"

"I won't if you have screen."

"Hold on. We might. Let me check our stock. This might take a while."

"That's fine, I'll wait."

Martin could hear the phone clunk down on the other end and could hear the clerk screaming out window screen questions to someone else apparently far away. In a few minutes the voice was back. "Yeah, we got screen, framed and in rolls."

"Great, I'll be there in an hour."

Martin copied down the address of the hardware store and thumbed through the book for art supply houses. He would need lots of plastilene, which held its shape better than clay. He could get some from the factory, but he didn't want to deal with Vicki, not now. And lighting? He'd call around. Maybe fiber optics for the internal glow, but who sold it? He started flipping through the Ls.

Chapter Eighteen

"AND SO I SAY to you, lift up your hearts and give thanks to the Lord, for though your travels take you far from home and from those you love, the Lord will be always there and will guide them lovingly in your absence. Amen," said the Reverend Barry Blackwell from the pulpit of the little mariner's chapel off the lobby of the Lutheran Seafarer's House.

"Amen," echoed the small congregation in a rough, self-conscious mumble from where they were peppered lightly across the pews. There was a spindly octogenarian seated to the left, second row back, head keeled over and snoring, and at the back to the right was a young Black boy, seemingly not more than fourteen. His large bright eyes were only one shade lighter than the brilliant dab of gold that dangled from his ear; he was trying his best to look like a seaman. Father Manoel was seated on a pew across from the boy, looking up to his friend with rapt encouragement. In fact, the only thing large about the congregation, other than the reverend himself, was Alf at the right front pew—who had already stood in anticipation of the hymn. He was heavy with ballast like a channel buoy in a rough seaway, and in his red sweater, he looked like a pear wrapped up to give a favorite aunt for Christmas.

"Let us rise and sing number 141 in our hymnals."

All stood, except the elder who was snoring.

The reverend and Alph commenced in sync, each trying to out blast the other in their dueling zeal:

> Rock of Ages, cleft for me,
> Let me hide myself in thee;
> Let the water and the blood
> From thy wounded side which flowed,
> Be of sin the double cure,
> Save from wrath and make me pure.
> Could my tears...

Father Manoel dropped out of the song at a touch upon his shoulder. Freddy, the desk man that day, had something to say.

"Yes Freddy?" questioned the priest, as quietly as possible.

"Somebody wants you on the phone. I knew you was in here, so I came over. You gonna take it?"

Father Manoel knew from experience that Freddy loathed to take messages and took pains to ensure that the ones he did take were vague and useless enough to discourage callers from leaving more in the future. Father Manoel didn't want to abandon his friend's sermon—he was a quarter of the congregation after all—but it might be important, so he picked up his coat and followed Freddy out. Alf and the Reverend Blackwell volleyed booming cannonades as they departed.

The phone was lying off the hook on the front desk, and the switchboard behind it was alive with blinking lights. Freddy let them blink.

"Hello, this is Father Teixeira."

"Hi, Father, it's Martin."

Good, he had finally called. Father Manoel had been waiting for a call for three days and had almost phoned the sculptor a number of times himself, but he thought it would be better to give the man his space and to pray for his success instead.

"Hello, my son. I was hoping to hear from you and have been praying for you. How are you?"

"Fine, Father. Good, thanks. I think that maybe your prayers paid off." There was excitement thinly hidden beneath his measured words. "Look, I want you to come over tonight as soon as it's dark. I have something that I think you'll want to see."

"You mean you've done it, Mr. Drake?" He crossed himself.

"That's your call, Father. Remember?"

"I'm sure it will be wonderful. I'm excited to see it."

"Well, come over then tonight, just after sunset."

"I could come right now."

"No, let's wait until dark. See you then. Bye." He hung up.

When Father Manoel placed the phone back in the cradle, one of the lights on the switchboard died, but neither he nor Freddy, who was reading a back issue of *The Seafarer's Log*, noticed . He returned to the chapel in time to catch the last verse of the second song:

> God protect the men who sail
> On merchant ships through storm and gale.
> Through peace and war their watch they keep
> On every sea in thy vast deep.
> Be with them God by night and day.
> For merchant mariners we pray.
> Amen.

Chapter Nineteen

"Good to see you, Father. Please, come in."

Martin ushered the priest into his apartment.

"Mr. Drake, I've been on pins all day since your phone call. You've done something that you like?"

"Yes, I have. I think I finally hit it this time, and I think you're really going to like it. I hope so, anyway."

The priest clapped his gloved hands.

"Are you cold or excited?" asked the smiling sculptor.

"A little of both. No. A lot of both. It's worse here at night without the sun to warm you. I didn't think it could get colder than it does in daylight, but it can. And I've been able to think of nothing but your statue since you called."

"I've got some coffee on, if you'd like some. The pot's been hot since I started working on this project of yours."

"Maybe later, my son, after we look at your masterpiece."

"Save that word until you see it, but come on, take a look and let me know what you think."

They walked down the shadowed hall to the studio, which was dark except for a faint loom, like reflected city lights viewed from forty miles at sea. The soft glow intensified as they drew near, and as they approached the threshold, Martin let the priest enter alone.

Father Manoel stepped through the sanctuary door and then stopped dead in the water, awed by the wonder expanding in his sight—it was a bust more noble than any chiseled of Hellenic marble. God rose radiant before him. His long hair and beard crackled in still air as if stirred by internal breezes, and his eyes beamed pure white light beneath the fineness of his brow. But even this regal visage, beyond all others the priest had yet beheld, seemed inadequate to hold for long the glory trapped beneath it, and even as he stared, it seemed to break apart. Seams of light, pure light, like that blazing from the eyes, broke through exquisite features in glowing, widening rifts. The beauty of the image seemed ready to explode from a power and might that could not be bound within, as if the wonder of this face beyond description was a thinly veiled travesty, a cheap facade wrought by a weak and feeble mind who thought, impiously, to picture God—a wildly impossible, impertinent dream.

Father Manoel knew at once that he was gazing upon a unique masterpiece. His feet drew him closer to the light.

The sculptor watched the priest stand before God, bathing in profound and humble adoration. He brushed Sharon's tears gently in the darkness and kissed her softly the cheek. Then he spoke across the silence of the void, "I'll start work on him tomorrow."

"THIS IS A PLASTER of Paris cast of the clay bust I showed you last week," explained the sculptor to the priest admiring his work. "Most people think that a bronze casting like the one you've contracted me to do is a simple process…one simply models the sculpture and then sends it off to the foundry to be bronzed. Well, it's not quite that easy."

"To be honest with you, Mr. Drake, I have no idea how a statue evolves, but there is nothing simple about what I see here. I can't fathom how you even thought of it, much less sculpted it. I have to admit that I envy your talent, though as a priest I suppose I shouldn't. And I shouldn't be telling you about it either. The only thing I can sculpt is triangles out of a cheese wheel, and they usually don't come out right."

Martin smiled warmly. "I'm glad to know of your envy, Father. If I can count that as a fault, I'm happy: it makes you seem more human and makes me more comfortable. Holy men make sinners nervous. I was beginning to think of you as some sort of avenging John the Baptist come up from the jungle to baptize me with fire. And you did too. I sweat some blood on your account, but you know what? It felt good. And stop calling me Mr. Drake. Call me Martin."

"And you can call me Manoel."

"Okay, Manoel, but Father suits you better. It fits. And who knows, once this is done, you might think the title 'sculptor' fits me too."

Father Manoel saw the confession in Martin's eyes. "I already do, my son—I mean, Martin. I knew you were a sculptor after I saw the pictures of your early work, and I'm glad you've come back to yourself again. Your gift is a blessing to be shared by many people."

Martin was touched but embarrassed, so he shifted away from the praise. It was enough to know the priest was satisfied with the work. He didn't need to hear any more.

"Now let me explain what we have ahead of us..."

"Please do."

"We're through the hardest part of the job—coming up with a working model that we're happy with. I nearly killed myself trying to get this one right. It was a little bit tougher than a knight on a horse, or a mayor or any of those other pigeon perches out in the park. This one took some thought. But it's finished, and we like it. So now we move on.

"As I said, this is a plaster replica of what I modeled in clay. I need to use a model now that will hold its shape through the enlarging process. The clay, plastilene actually, that I used to sculpt the original model was a little too delicate for enlarging, so we use plaster of Paris. This is an enlarging machine."

Martin placed his hand on a large wooden cantilevered arm projecting out from the tripod on which the plaster bust was set. On the far end of the arm pointing up to space was a metal pointer, and on the end above the bust was another pointer shaped in a crescent. The two pointers were joined through the articulated cantilever in a series of pulleys and graduated knobs.

"What this does is allow me to make an exact replica of the statue as an enlargement. I could also make a reduction, if we wanted one. It lets me get the proportions right without having to guess and basically re-sculpt the larger statue from scratch. It's sort of a three-dimensional template in space. I've already set it for an enlargement five times the size of the original. This plaster model is twenty-four inches high, so the final model will come to exactly 10 feet as you specified in our contract."

The priest nodded his understanding and asked to be sure, "So what you will do next is make a full-size clay model using this machine to guide you."

"That's right, but before I do that, I have to make an armature, or framework, to support it. That's what all of that steel and wire in the corner is for." Martin motioned to the heap. "I couldn't even sculpt the first scale model without an armature. There really isn't much clay involved in this sculpture at all, compared to most others. The form is built up from within. In this case, the armature is very much like skull and bone, and the clay is like skin. I would have built it up from a clay base if I could have, but the internal lighting I needed wouldn't let me get away with it. The statue had to be hollow for the light, and the clay had to be laid-on in pieces fit exactly to form the face, but with enough space between them to let the light escape and to give it the exploding effect that it has. So what I first have to do is build the armature. I saved the frame from the original model and will enlarge it, and then we'll start building up the clay. The armature on this piece is the key, but it shouldn't be too tough. I'll start it out with bendable eighth-inch wire frames with wire mesh overlay, and then I'll get inside after it's enlarged and beef it up with half-inch pipe stiffeners—it has to be rigid enough to hold the clay. Then finally, it will be time for the bronze.

"It sounds more involved than it is. There is a lot of metal in this armature, but it doesn't have to support that much weight. The layer of bronze will be thin. Other statues get trickier. Think of a pirouetting dancer, all arms, legs and spreading skirt, balancing precariously on a single toe—the weight of bronze resting on that thin toe can be enormous. Or think of a cowboy waving from the back of a rearing horse. Again, a ton or more of metal balanced on two thin hooves, with the man and horse bent back beyond the center. No, this won't be difficult. Tedious, maybe, but not difficult. Actually, I don't really mind this work. It's relaxing in a way, and we have the birth of the statue to look forward to."

"I had no idea that there was so much involved," admitted the priest, who looked dubiously at the sprawling enlarger and the odd pile of metal scraps, rolls of wire and boxes marked "plastilene," wondering how the sculptor was going to turn it all into a larger version of the bust before him.

The sculptor, who was animated with the task, seemed to want to share every detail of it. He talked on, "Well, we're not there yet. Once the armature is done, I'll enlarge each one of the pieces that form the face individually, will reinforce each with internal wire mesh and will then place them on the armature to check for fit. Once that's done, I'll send them to the caster who will, about a week later, return a jigsaw puzzle in plaster of Paris that I will reconstruct on the armature. Then, if they look good, we'll load them in a truck and take them to Queens to the foundry I use, and we'll have them cast in bronze. Finally we'll insert the lighting, attach the bronze skin, buff it clean, and then with the flip of a light switch, your face of God should come to life."

"I can't wait to see it, Martin. The small one is so powerful. The full-size bust will be fantastic!"

"We'll see. Now let me get started." Martin removed the bust from the enlarging machine and replaced it with the original armature. Then he swung out the cantilever to an area he had cleared on the studio floor. He moved back and forth between the armature and the work area, moving the arm in slight increments around the small frame and slowly chalking off the base of the large statue on the worn parquet tiles of the studio floor. There was a determined pleasure in his work, not concentration. This was easy for Martin, the priest could see, and he seemed to be enjoying the ease after the past two weeks of struggle. Martin was happy. He felt like talking.

"So, Father Manoel, tell me about your mission."

"It's not a mission, Martin. Foreigners have missions in Brazil, not Brazilians—I came with the territory. I direct a foundation which operates ten *crèches*..."

"What's a *crèche*?"

"Oh, I'm sorry that's the Portuguese word—nurseries. We take in the children of poor families for the day, so their parents can both work. The minimum wage in Brazil is about sixty-five dollars a month, depending on inflation, and the wage is usually varying down, not up. Even with two breadwinners, life is a challenge, but the extra money does add up: it occasionally puts a chicken in a pot otherwise filled with beans. And we feed the kids breakfast and lunch when they're with us and provide them with dental care. Some of these kids wouldn't eat otherwise. And see a dentist? Never. When poor children get a toothache, they struggle on alone, and if they get sick and eventually die, they are buried with little ceremony—their parents grieve, and life goes on."

"That's awful!" exclaimed the sculptor, looking up from his chalking on the floor.

"Yes, but life can be awful. God can sometimes be a hard taskmaster, but we must meet his tasks and carry through. He is wise and merciful, and there must be a reason behind suffering. Maybe by trying to end it, we are acting in accordance with his will."

Martin couldn't see wisdom or mercy in the suffering of a horde of hungry children, but he thought it noble that the priest had chosen to try to stem it. He spoke as he traced the segments through the chalk marks that encompassed him. "It sounds like a good thing you're doing, taking care of those kids and helping their parents."

"Oh, it is, I suppose, but that's nothing really. Trying to feed the starving children of the world is like...what was it Simon Bolivar said? Oh yes...'It's like ploughing the sea.' Hungry mouths breed hungry mouths, quick and in quantity. Keeping people alive but in poverty only leads to more poor people. No, it's good to know that the kids don't go to bed hungry at night, but that's not the true aim of my work: what we are attempting to do is to educate, and through education, we hope to break the chain of poverty."

"Yes, I remember that you send kids to school."

"That's right. That's the heart of my effort. I want to end illiteracy in my country, and I want to open the minds of children. Education is expansive. It's the key to unlock the door to a better future. We teach children first to dream, and then we give them a few basic tools to turn their dreams into reality: reading, writing, arithmetic— these simple things are ciphers to the ignorant. We want to erase ignorance. A twenty-year-old without a basic education is destined to scrape out his living toiling in somebody else's fields or to steal it from another. Slavery or thievery. What great options, eh?

"The church has been in the business of education for centuries, but unfortunately, its programs don't have much reach in the humbler segment of our population. I pray that this will change."

The sculptor shook his head as he worked upon the floor, where he was now laying out the steel angles that would form the base. He had never thought much about the street people who sometimes tried to sleep in a huddle on the stoop of his own building at night—until the doorman ran them off. They were just a nuisance, possibly dangerous, but hardly people to him. He never wondered why they were homeless. They had been sifted from society somehow. In America, everybody had a chance, but these kids in Brazil? They were cast from the chafing floor before the grain was threshed. He agreed with the priest: a little bit of education does make a difference. Would he have been a sculptor if he had never studied art? He marked an angle for cutting. What the priest was saying made sense. He looked up from his work. "So, you send your kids to school once they're old enough?"

"We try to. It's funny, but there is always some resistance. Some parents don't want their children to attend school. They would rather have them out working or hustling, anything to bring more money in. The cities in my country are full of little shoeshine boys whose kits are bigger than they are, who struggle along with their burdens in search of an occasional customer, and the streets are also lined with tiny thieves and teenage murderers. It's a sad thing. But we help as we can, and since we pay for the books and school supplies and since we feed the children in our care, most parents usually let us have them. The kids are happy too. The life of a student in a classroom is better than that of a pickpocket alone on the street at night.

"And this year will be a pivotal year for our program: our first graduates will walk down the aisle to pick up their high school diplomas. I was afraid that they might not make it because we lost our funding, but the money we raise with this statue will keep us alive for another few years."

"What happened to your funding?"

"It was given to another 'charity'."

"You sound sarcastic."

"Oh, I am, Martin. Sarcastic and angry. Maybe that's the problem with my country. We Brazilians get too sarcastic and not angry enough."

"Meaning what?" asked the sculptor, who had stopped measuring the iron angle on the floor at the change in the priest's voice.

"Well," said Father Manoel, "the politics in Brazil are less than clean. They are our great national joke. And unfortunately, most of the money for my foundation was directed through an office in government headed by the wife of the president. The former first lady took an interest in my foundation, studied our annual report and then decided that the idea was good, but would better serve the people of her home state, so she cut our funding and sent the money back home.

"That was three years ago. Since that time, the president resigned to save himself from impeachment on corruption charges, and it turns out that our wonderful first lady had been funneling our money to her family. She claimed it was all an honest mistake. The word for poor people in Portuguese is '*carentes*,' and the word for relatives is '*parentes*.' She thought the money for the '*carentes*' was meant for her '*parentes*.' An honest mistake, right?"

Martin laughed incredulously and asked, "She got away with that?"

"Of course! She hasn't been charged with any crimes and hasn't returned any of the money either. Oh that's nothing! Her husband stole over 250 million dollars, and now they're both in Miami, living like kings."

"I can't believe it."

"Believe it. In Rio, store owners lash out and hire assassins to kill child criminals who roam in robbing gangs and who our laws make it difficult for the police to arrest, but when it comes to presidents or congressmen robbing us blind, we laugh and let them go—nothing can be done because they have immunity in office, so we just sit back and joke about it and drink a beer, a big joke on us right? Immunity for the politicians, impunity for the wealthy and misery for the rest. The rich and the powerful are above the law in my country, and the poor are below it. "

"And what about your money now?"

"Another big joke. I have reapplied for our former grants, but they are all still frozen pending an investigation that hasn't even started yet, three years later. So there the money sits, in the former first lady's family bank accounts only God knows where and in government coffers, and the good things we are doing will fall to dust with nobody giving a damn at all until election time, when suddenly every little man is important, when promises rule the sky. Politicians' promises don't hold much for me."

Martin rose and walked over to the pile of metal where he grabbed another angle. He set it down inside his marks and asked, "So that's why you came up here, to get some aid money?"

"That's right. I came up here to speed through a UNICEF grant we've applied for. The UN moves a little faster than the Brazilian government, but it's not exactly an engine of efficiency. I've done all I can, and we will get the money eventually—but not before I would have had to suspend the operations of six of our nurseries. I have had good success with American Catholic charities. They've been generous, but it's not enough. I was agonizing over which centers to close and over which child's dreams to break, when Harry Banks approached me and offered his help. I have no idea how he found out about us, but he did. It had to be the work of God."

"Information comes easy to a man like that, Father Manoel," offered Martin.

"It doesn't matter—it's still a miracle. I think it's a miracle that Harry has come in time to save my *crèches*, and I think there's a miracle in your hands to let you sculpt what you have sculpted. And I hope in my own small way, by nudging you along, that I helped a little too."

"You have, Father. I would have never done this if it weren't to get you off my back." He smiled and looked to the priest. "This is as much yours as mine. If it weren't for you, I'd be sitting in some restaurant right now, hawking Vicki's mannequins to someone I thought an idiot for buying them. Not a bad job really, but I'm happier here, working for a change. Making instead of taking feels good. I want to see this thing finished."

"When you're done, Martin, are you going to go back to selling those mannequins again, or are you going to remain an artist and sculpt things like this?"

"I don't know," he replied honestly.

Martin stood and looked around to the work beneath his feet. The base frames were marked and in order. He was ready to cut. "Could you give me a hand moving these over to the bench?"

"Of course."

The men gathered up the steel and moved it, in two trips, to a workbench beside the welder. Martin unreeled a few loops of hose, opened the valves and then sparked alive an oxyacetylene burning rig. He quickly cut the steel with molten, efficient tongues of fire. Father Manoel watched him work, but had to look away from the intense flame that hurt his eyes and left in them little purple traces when he blinked. When Martin finished burning, he shut off the gas, drained the hoses and looped them back into their resting place.

"Let's move these back over. Careful. They're hot. Here, put on these gloves." He handed Father Manoel a pair of heavy welder's gloves, which felt stiff on his fingers when he put them on. They moved the steel back into the oblong that traced the shoulders of what would be God. Martin assembled the pieces in order, and they fit together as he had planned and hoped. Often in the past, he would eyeball a length and cut it, only to find that he had cut it too short when he was already deep into the project with new welds. He would then spend hours grinding out his mistakes. With clay he was a master, with steel he was not. He had since learned to use a tape measure, a practice that now saved a lot of time.

"Good, they fit. Now I'll just tack these together, and then we can go have lunch. I'm buying."

"Thanks Martin, but you don't have to do that."

"Come on Father, it's my pleasure, and the next time I get down to Brazil, you can take me out to lunch. Deal?"

The priest laughed. "Deal!"

Martin went over to the bench where he had cut the iron and began rolling out welding cable into his work area. Then he hopped back to the bench where he picked up his stinger, some rod, an old long-sleeve work shirt and his helmet. He bent down to set the welder's amperage and saw the ragged, sooty hole that he had blown through the top of it the night he was drunk and had first tried to work on the project. *Shit*, he thought, *I wish I hadn't done that. Now, I'll have to buy another one.* He'd get another welder delivered that afternoon. There wasn't much time to be wasted, and he wanted to make every day count. There would be delays of a week with both the caster and the foundry. I need one today, but who delivers welders? The phone book held the answer. In New York City, everything was but a call away. He put down his equipment and turned to the priest.

"I'll weld this up later. Let's go have lunch, but first, I need to make phone call."

As they walked out of the studio, toward the living room, Martin winked to the girl who walked away into her field of white.

Chapter Twenty-one

"A H, MR. DRAKE, HOW good to see you. It's been such a long time," said the fat Frenchman as he rushed over on thick, stout legs. "I thought that you had abandoned us."

"Never in a million years," answered the sculptor, who shook the fat man's hand.

"Father Manoel, this is Andre. He is the one responsible for this," Martin patted his belly.

"Please no! Don't insult me, Mr. Drake. I'm ashamed of you. Now this," he squatted just slightly and then with both arms hefted his distention, "is a belly. Come by more often, so I can beef you up. I am glad to meet you, Father." He shook Father Manoel's hand in his hearty paw.

"The pleasure is all mine," the priest responded.

"No. No. The pleasure is mine. Truly. Now please, come this way."

The Frenchman marched ahead and pulled a chair from Martin's regular table. He seated them, and with a curt wave of his hand, summoned the wine steward. "I will be back shortly to take your order. I'm so glad to see you have come back to us. You worried me these last few weeks." He clapped hands and was off to greet another patron.

The wine steward appeared with the wine list and Martin took it.

"Would you like some wine, Manoel," Martin asked as he studied the selection.

"No, no thank you, Martin. I don't often drink. Maybe just some water or some juice."

"Are you sure?"

"Oh yes, quite sure."

Martin closed the list and handed it back to the steward. "What kind of juice do you have?"

"Orange, tomato, passion fruit, carrot juice and lemonade."

"Lemonade would be fine," said the priest.

"Great, lemonade then, and a double Glenlivet, no ice."

"Of course, Mr. Drake." The steward was gone in an instant but was soon replaced by a waiter with their drinks and another carting breads and pâtés.

Father Manoel toyed with the intricate lemon peel and cherry garnish that spiraled from his tall, frosted glass, looking every bit like a jungle orchid. He looked to the china and the silver flatware before him.

"This is a very elegant restaurant," he said.

"I like it. I eat here three or four times a week when I'm not dining with clients. You're the first one I've ever brought here. I usually eat here alone."

"It must be terribly expensive."

"No, not really. I bought the meal plan."

"Meal plan? What's that?"

"Nothing, just a joke. No, it's really not that bad for what you get. What kind of food do you like, Father?"

"Oh just regular food. Rice, beans, meat, chicken. Anything, really. I'm not picky."

"Be careful when you say that around here. If you ask the chef for his suggestions, you'll be eating sautéed frogs' legs and dandelion roots."

"Frog legs?" asked the priest. "I've eaten them before, but never in a restaurant. But they would be fine. Anything would be good."

"That's okay, Father, we'll skip the weird stuff and eat good, safe food. I don't know if they have rice and beans, but I'm sure they'll have something you'll like. How's the lemonade?"

"It's wonderful."

"Good. Now here comes Andre with the menu."

"He doesn't have a menu."

"Wait and see."

"Are you gentlemen ready to order?"

"Sure Andre. What's on for today? Skip the frog legs, rabbits and snails, just meat, birds and fish."

"Well," said the *maître d'*, who felt cheated at not being able to offer the whole menu. "The chef has prepared some exquisite squab *forestière*..."

"No pigeons"

Andre sighed, "Mr. Drake, you don't know what you are missing. How can I increase your girth if you won't let me give you a proper selection?"

"You're doing just fine. Now go on."

Andre leaned back, took a deep breath and began to recite the long, delicious and edited menu, chock-full of so many adjectives and accents that it surely lost everyone on the first recital. The richness of his words was only overpowered by the message they conveyed. A smorgasbord of gourmet delights rolled before the diners in a meandering waltz of smells and sauces, teeming with leaping fish and swimming, quacking, roasted ducks. When it was finally over, Martin picked sliced veal, and Father Manoel, after continued prodding from the artist, chose boiled lobster, which he craved but thought too expensive. Andre motioned for a waiter, dictated their order, then swam away in his river of description.

"You'll love the lobster, Father. They fly them in daily from Maine. I've never had a lobster here that didn't weigh at least three pounds, full of meat too, not like those you sometimes get that are huge but hollow inside."

"You were kind to have insisted that I try it, Martin, but I feel guilty: it must cost a fortune."

"Why feel guilty? Somebody's gonna get him, so it might as well be you. And anyway, it costs a fortune sure, but not as big as the one I'm making off that statue. I'm getting rich off of you, so drop the guilt and pick up a breadstick—they're really good here."

He picked one up and crunched it in his mouth. The priest followed his lead and crunched one too.

"These are good—garlicky."

The priest swallowed and asked, "Do you have family, Martin? Any brothers and sisters? Parents?"

"Everybody does. Yes, I have a brother and two parents."

"Are they here in New York?"

"No, they're all in Smithfield, Massachusetts—western Mass."

"Is that far from here?"

"No, not far at all. You can make it up there in four hours driving fast."

"That's nice. Then you must see them often."

"I suppose I could, but I don't. I don't think I've made that trip in...I can't quite remember, but it's been at least five years."

"You're not close to your family?"

"No, not close at all."

"I'm sorry to hear that."

"Don't be. You don't know my family. We never got along. My father was a grocer—you know the story—the kind of guy that starts out with nothing, works hard all his life without ever getting very far and then decides to yoke his unrealized dreams on the backs of his kids and light their butts on fire, trying to launch them to the moon."

"He had great expectations for you?"

"He thought they were great, but I never did. He wanted to populate the world with boy athletes who would metamorphose into doctors and lawyers after winning their fourth consecutive state high school football championships. I didn't quite fit the mold. My brother did, though. He was four years older and was the football hero, all right. He managed to live through it without getting too addled, and now he's back in Smithfield, filling cavities in a strip mall on Highway Four. And now my parents get their teeth fixed for free. I think Mom and Dad were hoping for a brain surgeon, but they seem satisfied with the dentist—teeth go bad more often than brains, so they think anyway. They never really thought much of me. I never played football and didn't go to law school. I doodled my way through high school, but did well enough to earn a scholarship to study art here at NYU. Once I got to the city, I never wanted to leave for long. I think I was afraid that if I went up to Smithfield, I might have somehow gotten stuck there, held forever captive by the local version of the American dream, but I did go on occasion. I used to see my family for a week or two during summer vacations, when I wasn't down here working, waiting tables and doing commercial design for money to spend during the school year. It was depressing for me to go back even for a couple of weeks. In everything

I was always measured against the football-playing dentist. I was the family failure. It got old."

Martin took a swallow of whiskey then dabbed some goose liver on a roll.

"Try this, Father, it's good too."

The priest experienced the pâté.

"It is good. But Martin, surely you keep in touch. Your parents still can't hold your career choice against you. Look at yourself, you're famous."

"Yeah, I know. That's what kind of made me write them off, my parents I mean. I was never close to my brother. He was quite a bit older and too perfect to spend much time with me. I doubt if he even remembers me. Oh, I suppose he does. Now that I'm wealthy, my parents probably judge him the failure. But at least he does their dental work. They save there."

He took another drink.

"My parents wouldn't help me with college unless I changed my major, which I wouldn't do, and then when I graduated, the only thing they could do was try to push me out of art. They thought I was wasting my time. I showed them my work my entire life, but never got a single word of encouragement or praise, until I started making it big— then they were my greatest fans. The last time I went to Smithfield, they had all of the neighbors over to meet the famous sculptor and threw a big party. It got to me. I'd struggled all of my life to get under a spotlight, which they had always scoffed at, and then there they were, taking credit, bathing in the envy of their friends and basking in my glory. I never went back."

"I'm sorry to hear that, Martin. You should try to forgive them."

"Maybe I will. One day. What about you? Any family?"

"I'm a priest. The church is my family."

"Sure, but what about real family: mother, father, sisters, brothers."

"My mother died when I was five, and I never knew my father. I had a sister once, but I lost her long ago."

"She died?"

"Yes, I suppose she did. She probably did. I never knew for sure."

"How can you not know something like that?"

The priest pushed a bit of pâté around his bread plate with the tip of a silver butter knife. He seemed lost in sad memory. Then he looked up to the sculptor, whose brows were confused in interest.

"It's a complicated story."

"Well, I'd like to hear it, if you want to tell it to me."

"I'll tell you, Martin, but first, would you look at that lobster. It must weigh ten kilos. Look how big its feet are!"

"Those aren't feet. They're claws."

Waiters filled their plates with abundance. Martin's veal swam in a sea of wine and mushrooms. The mushrooms were large enough to house a flock of fairies under their puffy canopies, and Father Manoel's lobster threatened him with steaming claws that seemed yet full of life. He looked dubiously at the dreadnought before him, seeking an angle of attack. The waiter had left beside his plate an array of grapples and boarding hooks, but he seemed reluctant to toss a line, draw his cutlass and board that rusty ironclad.

Martin cut a piece of veal and slid it in his mouth, where it melted scrumptiously. Then he looked across the table at the baffled priest and asked, "You going to eat him or admire him?"

"I'm not quite sure how. We only eat the tails."

"These Maine lobsters have meat all over, especially in the tail and claws. Break off a claw and then crack it open with that claw cracker, the hinged thing."

Father Manoel did as he was told. With a snap, pink-fringed white meat fluffed out from a rift in the lobster's rusty, broken armor.

"Good, now pull out the meat with one of those little picks."

Father Manoel withdrew a hunk of meat and dipped into his dish of lemon butter. His eyes grew wide when he tasted it. "Martin, this is delicious!"

"Yeah, they're good aren't they? Now tell me about your family."

"Well," said the priest, after he swallowed and wiped a trace of butter from his chin. "I'm not sure of the beginning of our story, really. I was very young, but I do remember my mother, images of her holding me in her lap. The rest my sister told me, but she was also young, and vague. My memories go back to a favela in Salvador da Bahia, but my sister said that we were born in the interior of the Northeast, in an area called the sertão. It's an arid place. A desert, really. Often it doesn't rain there for years, and the people there are very poor. Clarissa, my sister, told me that she, my mother, my older brother and I moved to Salvador with a man who wasn't our father when I was still a baby, so he and my mother could find work. There is nothing in the sertão, except starvation and hard-baked earth, and it's common for people to migrate from there to the cities. It used to be an abundant land before the droughts came, but now there is nothing left except people without much hope."

He broke his lobster's back and dug into it. "My brother, João, died making the trip. I don't remember him at all, but Clarissa said that he was a happy boy who laughed a lot, even when he had nothing to eat. The man left us soon after we got to Salvador, so it was just my sister, my mother and I. I really can't remember very much about it, just images of sitting on my mother's lap and playing with my sister. Then one day, *Mamãe* got sick. She just lay in bed, sweating and shaking, holding us to her and praying to *Nossa Senhora*. Then she stopped praying and died. How we cried. We just held each other and cried and cried. It was just the two of us then. The neighbors got tired of the noise, I guess, and came into the house to see what was wrong. They buried her and fed us for a few days, but within a week, we were forced from our *barraca* by another family. I remember my sister fighting with the man who stole our house—she scratched and hit him, but he was big and just pushed her out. Our neighbors did nothing. There was nothing to be done. They couldn't even continue to give us food: they didn't have enough for their own children. Everyone was so poor. That man and his family moved into our shelter, and we moved out. Then we lived in the street."

"My God, Father, you actually lived in the street? Where did you sleep? What did you eat?"

Father Manoel cracked another claw. "Oh, we slept wherever we could, under bridges, in storm drains. We couldn't hold a good place for long. There were always others looking for shelter, and with my sister a girl and I so small, we couldn't put up much of a fight. Most of the other kids in the street frightened Clarissa: she was at that age in-between being a girl and a teenager and was becoming beautiful, so the boys began to take an interest in her, but she didn't yet know why. She was always fighting off some boy or other. I would try to help, but would just get knocked down—I was more of a burden to her than anything, somebody to look after and to feed when she could barely survive herself. She would have done much better on her own, but she never left me. We would huddle together at night, mostly in doorways, and sometimes I would dream about *Mamãe's* death and scream myself awake. But when I awoke, Clarrisa's arms would always be around me, to comfort me. She was always there, humming and lulling me back to sleep.

In the daytime we begged and stole things when we could, and we picked through garbage—there's plenty to eat in a garbage can, even in Brazil. I bet I could get fat around here."

Father Manoel laughed, then bit into a dinner roll.

"Well, we must have lived like that for about two years. It was hard, and cold at night—for a Brazilian anyway—and we were always hungry. But I had my sister, who was my life. She was enough. Then one night, late, I remember being awoken by headlights and the sound of a car door slamming shut. Streets are always punctuated by noise, a passing truck, a barking dog, late night revelers stumbling home, so I didn't usually pay much attention, but I remember so vividly the sound of those boots scuffing the cobbles, coming our way, the sounds that a drunk makes, but amplified by the late night quiet in the ears of a frightened child. My sister was yanked up to her feet and dragged away from me. The man—I couldn't even see him, only his boots and the fear in my poor sister's face—he hit her several times and threw her in his car. I tried to pull her out, but he punched me in the face and knocked me down. I got up, and he did it again. I was still on the ground when he put the car in gear and spun away. The last glimpse I had of my sister was of her screaming, her crying face pleading to me in the rear window of that car as she disappeared into the night. I never saw or heard of her again. Then I was alone."

Martin set down his knife and fork and took a drink. He had the look of a man confronted by a friend who confesses to dying. He was uncomfortable, at a loss for words and without the ability to ease the pain.

"Manoel, I don't know what to say. That's so sad. I'm sorry."

"Oh it's nothing, my son. She has been long in heaven. She was an angel then, and she is now. I know that. I shouldn't have told you. Now I've ruined your lunch."

"No, I'm glad you told me. I just don't know what to say to you. It's beyond my experience. You've suffered so much. I thought my childhood was tough."

"Nothing of that, Martin. The Lord gives each his burdens and each his joys. I'm a happy man, especially now that you have come into my life to help me and my children. And to feed me! *Ave Maria,* Martin, this is the best meal I have ever eaten in my life!"

Father Manoel sipped his lemonade.

"What happened to you then, Manoel?"

Martin picked up his fork and tentatively speared another chunk of veal, but it was tasteless to him. He had lost his appetite.

"Well, I cried for days. I know that. The rest is sort of a blur. I looked for my sister, but never found her. I don't know how much time passed, maybe a few weeks. Then one night I fell asleep on the threshold of a church, where the next morning I was found and awoken by a priest. He took me in and cleaned me up, then he sent me to a Catholic orphanage. Then I was a Catholic. I fought the brothers at first—I couldn't stay there. I had to leave and find my sister. One night after I had been in the orphanage for some time, I did manage to sneak out—but nothing was familiar: the orphanage was far from the streets we knew. She was lost to me forever, and I surrendered her then to God. The next day found me crying at the brothers' door. I never left again. I was home.

"I was heartbroken about losing Clarissa, but I liked the orphanage. We had beds with blankets and more food than I had ever eaten. It was nice to play with the other boys, but what I liked most about the orphanage was school. We were educated there. The brothers wanted us to learn, and learn I did. I wanted them to love me, so once I learned how to read, I became the best student in every class, reading everything I could get my hands on. I played when it was time to play, of course. We would play *futebol* until the sun went down whenever we could get away with it—I was *meio-campo*, a good one too—but reading was my one true love. Books were doors that opened to a world outside the orphanage walls. I learned about my people through Machado de Assis and Jorge Amado and about the world through writers such as Conrad, Tolstoy and Hemmingway. And I also read and learned about the dear church that took me to its bosom. I loved the beauty of the mass and felt the love of Jesus descend upon me and bathe me when I took the Eucharist. He was and is a presence I can feel. Life had been so cruel to us outside, but he and his church had rescued me and nurtured me. They loved me in a loveless world. I wasn't there a year before I knew my destiny: I wanted to be a priest, so I could share the word and the love of God that had saved my life. The years passed, and I grew into a man.

"You know, I don't really know how old I am: my sister told me I was five when our mother died, and I was put with the seven-year-olds at the orphanage—I was about their size. It doesn't matter. As soon as I graduated from high school, I entered seminary and was ordained while still a young man. I was so happy and proud to be a priest. I wanted to conquer the world with the cross. I think the happiest day in my life was my ordination."

He toyed with his gutted lobster while he reminisced.

Martin motioned to a waiter to remove their plates. His wasn't half-full, but he was through. After the plates were whisked away in a clinking flurry, others took their place. "Would you care for dessert?" questioned yet another waiter.

"Oh, please no," responded the priest. "The lobster was too much. But it was excellent, my son. You must tell that to the chef."

"Certainly, Father. He will be happy to hear it."

"Are you sure you don't want any desert, Father Manoel? Their citron torte is fantastic."

"No thank you, Martin, I don't care much for dessert. I never had sweets as a child, and now I find them too rich. I only like sugar in my coffee, but thank you anyway."

"I don't want desert either, thanks, but could you please bring us some espresso and the check?"

"Certainly, Mr. Drake." The water vanished, but was back in a moment with the coffee. Father Manoel stirred in four spoons of sugar.

"You do like it sweet, don't you?"

"Oh yes, it's a vice I suppose, but a national vice—all Brazilians drink coffee this way. Do you take sugar?"

"No, I restrict myself to other vices. Black coffee works best for me."

They both sipped from their supercharged thimbles.

"This is good, Martin. Most coffee here tastes like wash water—it's all so weak, but not this."

"Yeah, if you want coffee like this you have to go to a coffee house and ask for espresso. American coffee is weak. Big cups with nothing in them.

"So when you left the seminary did you always work with children, or did you do other things, like working in a parish?"

Painful memories bubbled up as the coffee trickled down.

"No, not always with children..."

Cooking fires flared from the dark spot in Father Manoel's heart. Howler monkeys howled and jumped, and macaws screamed from the darkened canopy above him. He could hear the lament of a dying, trusting people. He downed the rest of the coffee and prayed then for forgiveness and success. *Help me to help this man to find himself, and help me to help my children. Let me bring good into the world!* Tears welled, but he capped them quickly. After so many years, they came with a question: Would they ever stop?

"Are you okay, Manoel?"

"Yes, I'm sorry. I'm fine. It's nothing."

"No, I'm sorry. I shouldn't have pressed you about your family. You've led a hard life."

"No, not at all, my son. It wasn't that at all. Perhaps the richness of the meal overcame me for a minute, but I'm fine now. Should we be going back to work? Can I give you a hand this afternoon? I'm free."

"No thanks, Father. I'm waiting for my welder, but I appreciate the offer. Come by tomorrow if you'd like, if you have a chance. I'd like you to see your statue come to life. I think you might enjoy it."

Martin paid the check, and the two men rose and walked to the door. They were greeted by Emily Buckman, who was just coming in.

"Why, Martin Drake, here you are again!"

Martin flinched at the sight of her. "Hello, Emily. How are you?"

"Just fine, and you?"

"Great. Emily, this is Father Manoel Teixeira. He's a client. Father, this the Emily Buckman."

"Nice to meet you, Father."

"And it is nice to meet you, Mrs. Buckman."

She smiled and looked to Martin.

"You're working for the church, Martin? I'm surprised. After hearing Amanda's description of your exhibition, I thought you'd be working for the devil himself."

Martin, for once, was at a loss for a retort, but Father Manoel came to his rescue. "I know what you mean, Mrs. Buckman, but I must tell you that this man is full of surprises. The bust that he is sculpting for me is magnificent and will be his redemption. You have only to see it to agree."

"Hmm, redemption for young Martin, Father? I must be getting even older than I thought. I certainly didn't expect to live to see that."

"Wait and see. It will be a masterpiece!"

"You must show it to me, Martin. Once again, you've intrigued a Buckman girl."

"As soon as I'm finished, Emily. I'll let you know."

"Good. Well, good to see you, Martin. Father, keep working miracles."

She moved to meet the beaming Andre while Martin and Father Manoel walked out to the street.

Chapter Twenty-two

MARTIN DREW THE POINTER on the small arm of the enlarging machine to a corner of one of the plaster squares forming the cheek of the model, then he climbed up the scaffold next to the full-size armature to check its placement: it was as it had been when he'd checked it the first time—right on. He was ready to mount the piece.

Martin climbed down and selected a square from the dozens laid out on drop cloths that lined the floor along the studio's walls. Holding its pliable form as a mother would hold an infant, he moved to the scaffold, and with utmost care, climbed up to the mesh base of the cheek. He checked the piece by eye to ensure that it wouldn't go on backwards like several others had before it. Satisfied, he laid it on and wired it in place. *Perfect.* Now on to the next one.

Martin swung himself back to the model and moved the enlarging machine's lower pointer to another neighboring patch, then climbed back up to note the position of the upper arm. Up and down he went to check each placement. *Good.* Nothing had changed. It was a painstaking process and slow, but it was worth taking a little extra time now to save being forced to take a lot of extra time toward the end of the project when things started not to fit. Problems multiply. But this statue was right on. Martin stepped down and hopped to the floor, searching for the piece. There it was, at Sharon's feet, amid a dozen others. As he picked it up, he patted her foot, then moved back up the scaffold as fast as caution would allow. He was checking it against its spot, seeking its exact alignment when someone started knocking on the door. *Shit.*

The knocking did not abate as he pondered whether to ignore it. Reluctantly, he lay down the plastilene swath carefully on the scaffolding, then climbed down and walked out of the studio to the front door. He squinched out the peephole but could see only a blur. Whoever it was, was standing too close. Maybe it was Father Manoel. He often spent time in the studio now, and strangely enough, Martin had come to enjoy his company. He would be happy with the progress made since yesterday. Martin hadn't been able to sleep the night before, so he turned his sleeplessness into work and felt more rested through the effort. His friend would be pleased. Martin swung the door open to a shock.

"Deborah!" *God, not now! I have to get rid of her.*

"Hello, Martin, may I come in?" she asked, as she passed by him. "Where have you been? You were supposed to come over to position my martyr for me. Remember? It's been over three weeks, yet I've heard nothing from you."

Emotion leached up her face like coal oil up a lamp wick.

"I know you don't like people calling here, but I was desperate to see you, so I called and left a few messages. Then I called again but got nothing. Your phone is disconnected. What's wrong, Martin? Are you avoiding me?"

Of course I am, he thought. He had been dodging her for years and was rather good at it, but this wasn't intentional. He had totally forgotten about her. He was too absorbed in the statue to remember his other mounting problems.

"I'm sorry, Deborah. I'm not avoiding you. I've just been so busy on the commission I'm working on now that I've pretty much neglected everything else, including you too, I guess. I'm sorry."

"Why didn't you return my calls? I left messages."

"I haven't even listened to my messages. Armine's been hounding me lately, and I just don't have the time to listen to her, so I turned off the machine. If it's really that important, she can drive over and beat on the door like you just did."

He grinned. She didn't.

"Honestly, Deb, I'm sorry. I wasn't neglecting you."

Her lips still pouted, but she moved closer. Then she grabbed him, her hands clutching bunched-up shirt cloth, which tugged it tightly across his back. Her head buried sobs into his lower chest.

"I missed you so, Martin. When my statue came and you didn't, I was heartbroken. I know you don't love me—I don't know if you ever did, but I still love you. I need to see you, at least once in a while. I know you only use me, Martin, but that's enough. Use me, but don't abandon me. I can't bear that. Please don't abandon me!"

Her words broke into sobs that pelted him in storms of pitiable misery.

He brushed the hair at the back of her head. *Poor girl.* Well no, not girl. She was much older than he. But there had been a time when he'd wanted her for something other than her money. Now look what had become of it. *Poor, poor girl.* She really was a girl, a simple, good-hearted girl trapped in an aging body and in a world that spun too fast for her.

Her tears marked his shirt and moistened the mat of hair beneath it. He hugged her to him and comforted her. He had become sarcastic and mean, but the worse he was, the more she wanted him. He didn't understand why anyone would want him really, not anymore, not since he had sold himself. But year after year, there she was with her heart and her purse in hand, offerings to the high priest of abuse, offerings to the devil. Poor sad eyes. Poor sad Deborah.

"It's okay, Deb. It's okay. It's all right."

Martin knew he had no reason to detest her as he had over the past several years. No reason at all. She had always been good to him, supporting his art and giving him affection when he'd needed it—long ago when he was heartbroken. No, he never loved her like she loved him, but there was a time when he did like her and was attracted to her. He looked down to the woman who had once been beautiful and remembered her that way. She had been so pretty then. Pretty, friendly and loving, but dumb like a puppy, always bubbling with enthusiasm for his work, which he thought ridiculous. How she encouraged him. How she bought from him. How she gave herself to him, taking risks to come when she shouldn't have. She would have done anything for him. He remembered how cute she was, lying with him in his studio, staring up at his contraptions as if she could see something in them, something never there. Her age and her obsessive want drew forth his revulsion, but he swallowed it back down. She had once been a friend. He didn't want to hurt her anymore. Why, he didn't know.

He lifted up her chin and wiped away her tears. "I'm sorry, little Deb. I should have called. I've just been so busy, lately. I'm working on a big commission against a deadline, working day and night. Would you like to see it?"

She looked up to him through her misery, studying him, half expecting a trick. Seeing no malice, she tentatively nodded yes.

"Come into the studio. I'll show you." He took her by the hand, led her in and guided her to the scale model on the pedestal of the enlarging machine.

"This is a bust commissioned by Harry Banks for a Catholic charity in Brazil."

"I didn't know he was Catholic."

"I don't know if he is Deb, but he's doing this for charity. It's the face of God."

She looked at it, but was still too hurt to be encouraging.

"It's very nice."

She looked back up to the artist, hoping desperately that he would hold her and help her ease her pain.

He pressed her hands and asked, "Remember Deb, when I was a poor nobody? Remember when you used to come into my studio and watch me work?"

"Those were some of the best times in my life," she whispered, as her tears began to run again.

"Would you stay with me today, Deborah, just for a little while? If you don't have somewhere else to be? Sit and watch me like you used to. I would like that."

"You would?"

Hope and doubt rang in her words.

"Yes, I would. Sit here."

He cleared a spot for her to sit beside his worktable. Then he kissed her forehead and sat her in a chair.

"Now, I'd better get back to work."

Traces of love glinted in her drying eyes as she watched him climb up the scaffold, where he knelt to pick up a piece of plastilene skin lying before the eyes of the giant. As he rose, he caught a glance of Sharon as she walked away. He shrugged at her, then turned to lay the patch.

Chapter Twenty-three

A T A BELL TONE, the floor grew heavy beneath Father Manoel's feet, and then with a jolt and the sliding of a door, all was right again. He stepped out of the elevator onto Martin's landing, as rich in statuary as a hotel lobby and as repellent as a carnival side show—a casualty of Mad Martin's reign as prince of a lower kingdom that he had hacked for himself from the spacious hinterlands of contemporary art. As he passed the looming, leering hulks, gargoyles of the new church, Father Manoel clapped his frozen hands and blew on them with futile breath. Nothing of acclimation in him, he was as frozen now as he had been when he stepped off the plane two months before. It was summer in Brazil, his heart lamented. He pulled off a glove and strained stiff fingers into an icy knocker, but the door swung open before he had a chance to use it.

"Hello, may I help you?"

"Hi, I'm Father Teixeira. I came to see Mr. Drake," he said, wondering who the woman was.

"Oh, you must be the priest working with Harry Banks. I'm Deborah Mondain." She held out her hand, which he shook. "Martin's working very hard for you, Father. I haven't seen him like this in years. It's a nice surprise."

"That's good to hear."

"He's in the studio now, working. Would you like me to tell him you're here?"

"No, that's all right, thank you. He's expecting me. I'll just walk in. I know the way."

"Oh, okay. Well, I'm on my way out. It's nice to have met you, Father." She flashed a smile, which he returned.

"The pleasure's mine."

They passed each other, he into the living room, she into the landing and its nightmare.

Father Manoel found Martin atop his scaffold laying on a clay patch with outstretched, caring hands, a Lilliputian surgeon attending a battered Gulliver . After the graft was on, he looked down to his volunteer assistant. "Hi, Manoel. I'm on the forehead already! We'll be ready for plaster tomorrow. Hey, could you hand me that spool of wire, there on the table, and those needle nose too."

Father Manoel picked up the sutures and handed them up to him.

"That's wonderful, Martin. You're really making progress aren't you?"

"Yeah, we're moving right along. No problems yet."

Martin knocked on the wooden platform as he kneeled down to grab the wire.

"Didn't see you yesterday, Manoel. You missed the nose go on."

"I know. You told me that that would be tricky. I meant to stop by in the afternoon, but I was at the UN all day chasing papers. At least the bureaucrats here show up to open their offices on time, but I don't see much difference between them and our functionaries back home. Nothing moves, except me, back and forth, back and forth between offices, smiling and nodding and waiting for somebody to get up and do something. These bureaucrats don't stamp things as much as ours do, though. The Brazilian government's built on stamps. *Carimba!*"

He pounded a fist into an open hand.

"Everything needs lots of stamps, ribbons too if they're warranted, but lowly paperwork like mine rates only stamps."

"There won't be much paperwork involved in this grant from Harry Banks will there?" asked the healer, as he wired in a stitch.

"No, not on this end, but in Brazil, *Ave Maria*, I don't even want to think about it. I'll spend weeks accounting for this money before they liberate it. Everyone is sympathetic. Everyone is understanding. But nobody knows anything, and nothing ever moves! I'll get the money cleared in time though. The Lord is on our side, Martin. Look how fast you're moving. His hand is on your shoulder."

Martin didn't feel a hand on his shoulder. He wanted to, but he didn't. He did feel, though, if there was a God, that he wouldn't find fault in this statue. It was good, and Martin knew it. But there was something missing. Something wasn't quite right. Where was the feeling of knowing he had hit it? This wasn't God. He couldn't quite see the spirit that he sought. But who could picture God? It was ridiculous, like grade school cowboys out at night, twirling lassos and trying to rope the moon. He shook away the thoughts that nagged him. The work was good, and that was enough.

"Hey Manoel, see those clay pieces over there, by Sharon?"

"Who's Sharon?"

"My statue."

"Oh."

Father Manoel looked over to the girl who walked away. She was walking away from a minefield of mud. Clay patches surrounded her in a jigsaw pile of pieces. "Yes, I see them."

"Well, would you go over there and bring me the one just in front of her?"

"Of course." Father Manoel walked over and examined the broken puzzle. "Which one?"

"The one right in front of you."

"This one?"

"No, the one next to it, right there by your foot."

"This one?"

"Yeah, that one."

Father Manoel knelt down and gently lifted the piece that wilted with his touch like a coral head brushed by a careless diver.

"Be careful with it, Manoel. They're thin."

"I'm being careful!" As Father Manoel lifted the piece, he caught sight of a bronze heel and admired the girl as he rose. She was so beautiful, such a lovely, tragic beauty. He still wanted to wipe away her tears. The bust that Martin was creating was monumental, a triumph, a masterpiece. But where it awed and overwhelmed with the clarion call of Judgment's trumpet, Sharon struck at softer chords. She plucked the heart strings in sorrowed strains of broken love and sundered dreams. He pondered her as he walked back to the artist.

"Martin," he asked, as he handed up the piece, "who is Sharon?"

The sculptor stooped, accepted the piece and held it as he looked down to his friend. "She was a wonderful person, Father Manoel. Sweet, honest, beautiful. She was the only woman I ever loved."

"Why did she leave you?"

Martin sighed, which spawned a little half-smile of regret.

"You shouldn't have to ask that. You know me well enough."

"You are a good man, Martin. You didn't seem one when I met you, but I know you now."

"She did too. That's why she left."

Martin laid the clay down carefully on the scaffolding, then swung his legs out to take a seat. He looked over to Sharon, sad at the sight of her still leaving. "We met in college, in a design class. She studied advertising, and I studied fine arts. A few of our courses overlapped, so that's how we met. It's funny. Nowadays, I'm a reputed scoundrel, always in the paper for some minor scandal or other involving a woman, but back then I was really more interested in my work. I was too busy and too intense to give girls that much thought. I was at odds with my professors and was forever getting into arguments over art. Same as now...when I gave them what they wanted, I got an A. When I gave them what was right, I got a C. But in those days, truth for me weighed more than success, so I swallowed the C grades, but not without screaming about it. Anyway, I made noise, and Sharon noticed. And once she got to know me and my work, she took my side. She believed in me. We dated through college and started living together as soon as we got out. We worked down on Madison Avenue. She was designing magazine spreads and I was drawing whatever hokey thing my bosses wanted to insert in the minds of demanding kids to sell to their appeasing parents. Then, after surviving those horrible days of doodling for dollars, we'd come home, eat dinner, love each other quickly, and I would sculpt myself into exhaustion until the early hours of the morning while she watched and talked to me. No TV for her: I was her distraction, and she and my work were mine. After a couple of years of this, she was promoted and was making decent money, enough for the two of us to live on, so she convinced me to give up commercial art and to concentrate on sculpture. And that's the way we lived for another two years, the happiest years of my life. We would wake up early, make love..." He blushed. "Sorry Manoel. I guess I shouldn't be telling you that."

"It may surprise you to know that I know all about those things, Martin. People are people, and that's how people make more people. It was God who told Adam and Eve to 'be fruitful and multiply and fill the earth.' Love is not sinful, not true love. But anyway, I've heard it all in confession. I could tell you things that would make you blush redder than you are now. Nothing's wrong with what you did. Love's a beautiful thing. It's something I have never known, and maybe that's a regret of mine. I don't know. But it's always a pleasure to see young people in love. Now go on."

"Okay."

Martin felt uncomfortable talking about himself to a priest. He had led a life far from the Christian ideal, but still, Father Manoel had become someone he liked to talk to. There was a lot beneath the clerical black—he was talking to a man.

Martin continued. "We'd get up, make love. Then she'd get dressed and rush to catch an uptown train, always almost late, leaving at the last minute, and I'd go into my studio where I'd work until she came home to me. Then we'd fix dinner and be together until she left again. It was a little less hectic then. I didn't have to stay up late into the night working, but I often did. When something was in my blood, I just had to get it out and could be hard to live with until I did. She was always understanding and never complained once—she said she liked to see my wheels spin. On weekends, we'd spend our mornings in bed and our afternoons and evenings in parks, museums or galleries. My life fell apart because of one of those visits."

"How so?"

"It's laughable, but it's the truth: I made my fortune and lost my love on a ten-dollar bet."

Martin looked sadly to the statue of the woman he loved; she was still bent on leaving.

Father Manoel watched him, drawn into the story, waiting, wanting to hear more.

Martin swung himself from his seat upon the scaffold and walked over to the statue. The priest followed. Martin brushed her cheek softly, then continued, "It seems so silly now doesn't it, sweetheart, but it happened. And we can't turn back the clock, not now. Too late was long ago."

He turned to the priest. "She's gone forever, and it was my fault. I made this statue to remind me of how she looked when she left. I don't know why, really. Maybe I wanted to have this image of her always, so I'd never forget the regret for having lost her. I wanted to suffer for it."

"Tell me what happened."

"Like I said, it started with the bet. One day we were making the rounds, visiting the galleries down on 57th Street, and I was getting miffed at what was selling—free-form abstracts were the rage back then. You know, like my work in steel that you hate, junk welded up any old way and then mounted. Some of it was good, truly art, but most of it was not. It was everywhere, exhibited in galleries by owners who wouldn't even let me in the door with my portfolio. I was getting angrier with every step. I was an expressionist then—I still am mostly, though what I've been expressing lately is just contempt—but at the time, I was sculpting people, trying to get at what was inside them, their motivation, what they were. It's exhausting work, really. You put a little of your soul in every piece, but that junk in the galleries was just plain junk, pure and simple, nothing abstract about it.

"I was going off at Sharon, raging on and on about how worthless it was, and how I could run off something like it in a day. She calmed me down, agreed with me, then made a teasing bet: ten bucks that I could do as well as anybody on exhibit and that she could sell it for me. We shook on it. Since we didn't have anything planned the next day, Sunday, I called around to some friends of mine when we got home and managed to both borrow an arc welder and get a quick lesson on how to use it. That Sunday, I piddled away the afternoon, welding things like we had seen the day before. When they were done, Sharon painted them and took pictures. That week after work she visited a few galleries and guess what—the gallery owners liked what they saw. Sharon had my work placed in just a week! People were fools. We had our proof. I had only managed to get four of my expressionistic sculptures on display in my entire life, and only two of them sold. Remember those bronzes that Armine showed you, which you thought were good?"

"The twisted people?"

"Right. In four years of sculpting, they were the only things I had managed to sell. Two sold. Two were returned to me, and the ones that sold, didn't sell for much. But all that junk I welded, six small figures, moved within a few months. Can you believe it? After my success, I was invited to meet a few gallery owners, and by the end of the year I was welding junk full-time.

"I wasn't thrilled with being a junk man at the time, but was earning money, and that was important to me. I needed to. Sharon had been the one supporting us for so long that I felt I had to give something back, and I was. I grossed more than she did within a year of her sale of those first abstracts. Well, we were still happy, not as happy as we were before because of my constant grumbling about my work and the stupidity of the society that valued it, but happy still. I continued to sculpt the things I believed in at night, but that got harder as time went on because of the workload the galleries imposed on me. It was around this time when I met Armine Quadras, and when things really began to change.

"She was and is a real hustler, and she saw a chance to profit off of me and my work, so she pushed me to sign her as my agent. I thought that an agent would be a good thing to have and hoped that she could sell the expressionistic sculpture that I couldn't. We spoke about my frustration at not selling my good stuff, and about having to sacrifice my work on it in order to pump out the abstracts that were paying the bills, but she told me not to worry, that once I was established she'd see to it that the galleries would start moving all of my work. She said that one day, after the abstract wave had passed, I'd be able to move back into expressionism. She would do the legwork and sales, so I could have more time to sculpt. It didn't quite work that way though.

"She was something then—you should have seen her. She didn't yet have her gallery and was working as a freelance publicist, advertising exhibition openings. She'd only been in business a few years, but she was hungry and already had connections. It's no wonder, the way she operated. Night and day she was on the run, bumping into everyone that mattered with her calculated magic and selling them what they wanted. Not art, not sculpture, no, not that at all. She was selling stardust—glitter and gold with a camera flash and the tinkle of champagne bubbles on fine crystal. Since I was young and handsome at the time, and could pop-out reasonable copies of the trash then popular, she thought I had promise. She thought I was another trained bear for the circus she was forming, and she was right. Before I knew it, the tent was raised, and I was center ring.

"She was incredible. She could see inside of people and divine their secret wants. People are books to her, books with bank accounts. We gave them what they wanted, and they paid good money for it. I found out quickly what Armine knew all along: the crowd we were dealing with wasn't much interested in art—our exhibitions were just sets for the soap opera of their lives, and we were just bit players. But it paid. How it paid! Though it also had its price. As I grew into the role of the jet set artist, my relationship with Sharon grew strained, and my art suffered too.

"I'm sorry to hear that," said the priest.

"It happens. Sharon got tired of the exhibitions, the continuous string of cocktail parties and all the paper smiles. She wanted to turn our life back to the way it was before, but I was getting hooked. I liked the praise heaped on me by the art critics we were pumping, and I liked the money and the growing notoriety. I liked being sought out by people who thought me a good artist. I had lost sight of the fact that the art they liked was like garbage to me, and as I became more successful, our carefully crafted sham slowly started working on me as well as our customers. I began to believe I was the man in the tuxedo, the boy genius with a welding rod, and I began to believe that my abstracts were real art.

"Sharon started staying home, sick of the people we dealt with, and growing sick of me and my inflated ego. We started fighting. She reminded me that I detested the kind of work I was doing and told me I was losing myself, that I wasn't the same man she met in college. But I wasn't listening. I was too caught up in the illusion to hear her, and if she didn't like the way our lives had turned out, it was her problem—she had become small minded. Maybe she just didn't understand my art. I went out night after night while she wouldn't, and with the glitter and the praise came other women. Why did I have to go home to fight all night with Sharon, ever more distant in an angry bed, when I could go off with those exciting, rich women who were throwing themselves at me? I started sleeping around. Armine encouraged it. She thought it was good for business, and it was.

"My reputation soared at the hint of scandal, and I was getting laid by a larger circle. And what's more, these same pretty women were buying my sculpture, paying us more and more as time went on. Armine understood it all so well. I think she knew when she signed me that I would become part of the package. It just took her a little while to work me into her system.

"Well, it couldn't go on forever. Something had to break, and Sharon finally did. One afternoon she came back from work in tears. She had seen a picture of me in the paper with another woman, Deborah Mondain." Martin stopped speaking for a moment. "That's funny, you know she was just here."

"I know," said the priest, "I met her as she was leaving."

"Did you? Yeah, she's been over here a lot lately, watching me work. I don't pay much attention. She used to really bother me. I guess in a way, I blamed her for Sharon's leaving, but it wasn't her fault. It was mine. Poor old girl. I was so mean to her over the years, but she always took it, ready to do anything for me whenever I asked her. Still is. I don't like her around and wish she wouldn't come, but I've hurt her enough and just don't feel like doing it anymore. She's harmless.

"Anyway, I was in the paper, arm around Deborah, and Sharon had had enough. I think that she suspected that I was fooling around for some time, but she chose to ignore it. The picture seemed truth enough. She asked the question, and I confessed. It destroyed her. She cried for hours, and there was nothing I could do to comfort her. When I tried to touch her, she cursed me and pushed me away. Finally, late that night, she pulled herself together and started talking. She said that she didn't want to leave me, but that she couldn't live like we were living anymore. A few weeks earlier, she had been offered a big promotion with a transfer out to the West Coast, which she hadn't even mentioned to me. Initially, she had turned it down because she didn't want to interfere in my career, but was reconsidering because of what I had done to our relationship. She threatened to leave me, but then changed her tune and pleaded with me, kneeling at my feet, crying and begging me to get away from this city and to go out west with her—where we could have a fresh start, away from the people who were pulling us apart.

"I don't think I'll ever understand what got into me that night—maybe it was the line of all those retouched Barbie dolls in evening gowns waiting for a crack at me, all dressed in shimmery silks while Sharon was forever in blue jeans and a T-shirt. Maybe it was the fact that of all the people I associated with at that time, she was the only one who didn't see my greatness. She had stopped believing in me, and I was so lost in my delusion that I couldn't see that she was right. I told her to go to California and take the job. I told her to leave. She did, and was in L.A. two weeks later. I didn't try to stop her. She came back to our apartment once more, the night she left, to ask me to give us another chance, and again came the ice: I told her no. I told her to get out and go."

As Martin wiped the bronze tears of the love he lost, his eyes welled. Ten years later, he was finally crying.

"What you see here, Manoel, was the way she looked as she walked out our door that final time. I never saw her again."

"I'm sorry, Martin."

The priest put a strong hand upon the sculptor's shoulder.

"I am too. I've never been able to forgive myself for hurting her or for letting her go—or for ruining my life. We had six wonderful years together, and I just threw them away in some awful cloud of self-deception. I couldn't see who loved me or who I loved. I couldn't see anything through the fog I was living in, and when I finally opened my eyes, I found that I had lost both my love and my art. I had lost it all."

"Did you ever try to contact her, Martin? Did you try to get her back?" asked the priest, as Martin stroked the monument, awakening to the tragic moment in which he still was living.

"I did, but not at first. I was angry with her for leaving, as if it were her fault for not understanding my new and elevated place in the world. If she had supported me and stood by me, then I wouldn't have needed other women, right? I thought that she was stupid to have left me. She was the one at fault, not me. No, at that point, I felt tremendous pain, but still couldn't see the cause of our break up. I felt jilted and tried to ease my pain by sleeping around with more and different women. Armine was all for it. She'd line me up whenever I needed a date. It took me a while to realize that there was nothing in it for me, just the flesh of strangers and a growing emptiness inside that only Sharon could fill. I tried to ease my pain by going more and more wild. That's when I really started drinking heavily. I snorted quite a bit of coke too, but booze was my main medicine. Life became sort of a blur, yet I was getting more and more successful. I can barely remember those days—round and round I went. I became a whore, in art, in body and in soul. I was negotiable. I was up for sale."

The sculptor leaned his head on the cheek of bronze. His tears mixed with hers.

The priest squeezed his arm and said, "Martin, listen to me. What you did before is history. It's good that you recognize your sins, but they're all in the past. Now learn from them and move on. Forgive yourself. God forgives. You must learn forgiveness too."

"A guy like me doesn't have much to do with God, Father, and I doubt that he wants to have much to do with me. Anyway, I don't want his forgiveness, and I don't want mine. I had everything, and I threw it away.

"I did try to get her back, though, after several months had passed. I talked to Sharon many times, but I handled it all wrong. I was always drunk when I called her, usually after having been out with a woman I didn't love who only served to make me terribly lonely for her. I'd call her up in the middle of the night and beg her to come back to me. She listened at first. She still loved me then, but there was nothing she could do—she was obligated to keep working in L.A., and she wasn't willing to quit and come back to New York, not if I was still on the party circuit. I was the one who had to make the move. She wanted me to go out to her so we could have a fresh start, but I wouldn't do it. My career was taking off, and I wouldn't quit, not then. I was still too wrapped-up in the show we were putting on to see that she had been right all along.

"I'd give it all away for another chance with her, but it's too late. I kept calling, drunk, getting nowhere and only prolonging her misery. Finally, she asked me to either come to her or quit calling. I fought with her, and she hung up. When I called again, her phone was disconnected. Some years later, I learned that she had married. I lost her, Manoel. I lost the one love I ever had in life, and it was all my fault."

The priest patted his shoulder and said, "You must quit dwelling on your past. Put it behind you."

"I try. I put her out of my mind as much as I can, but she always comes back to me, even now. A week doesn't pass without her coming to my dreams. Those dreams I have of her were what finally made me aware of what it was I lost—not just her, everything that meant anything to me. The dreams are always the same—she returns to our old apartment where I am working on an abstract, the one I welded up for her on that bet. She watches me work, and then she looks to a corner of the studio where my good sculptures are all smashed and piled in a heap along with photographs of the two of us and an old teddy bear I gave her. When she sees the pile she starts to cry, then turns and begs me to stop what I'm doing, but I won't stop. Finally I get mad and push her to the floor, where she lies crying. I work on, ignoring her, until slowly, sadly she gets up and walks out, stopping at the door to look back. The dreams always end the same way, with her looking back as she walks away, just like she's doing here. This is all I have left of her."

Martin turned to Father Manoel and grinned sadly. "All my success hasn't brought me much happiness has it, Manoel?"

"It doesn't seem as if it has, my son. But every day is a new day. You should put this behind you now."

"Maybe you're right. You know, when I finally realized what I lost, I never wanted to be happy again, not really. I didn't want to share myself with another person like I did with her. Maybe I didn't think I could. And I never really wanted to be an artist again, either. I guess I blamed the world for what happened to us, the art world anyway, the society set, the women I saw, like Deborah. That's what unnerved me so when I met you. You saw through me all along..."

"I didn't see through you, Martin," responded the priest. "No. When I first met you, I thought you were just some unscrupulous man, getting rich by shocking people. I didn't think you were an artist at all, but now I know different."

"But you were right. That's exactly what I am. I've done everything that you accused me of. Remember when you accused me of making a joke out of my art to see how far I could go and to see how ridiculous and gullible people could be by accepting it and buying it?"

"Yes, I remember. That's what I told you the night before you agreed to accept the commission."

"Well, that's exactly what I've been doing all these years, and people are truly ridiculous, aren't they? I guess I didn't ever want to sculpt another piece that either she or I would like. I didn't want to do anything good. I wanted the world to pay for our break-up by turning mansions and museums into junkyards. I've done well. Don't you think so?"

Father Manoel laughed and said, "Well, if that's what you were after, I must admit that you are a great success."

He paused for a moment, then he asked, "Martin, why did you accept the commission?"

"Why? A million dollars, that's why. I'm a whore, remember?"

"No, that's not what I meant. I mean why did you change your mind that night and agree to work on it yourself?"

"Well, Manoel, you were the first person I've met since Sharon left with balls enough to tell me that my work is

189

trash, and you were the only person other than Sharon who appreciated the few sculptures I did that ever meant anything to me. You made me feel like trying again, and maybe like living again a little too. Sharon would have liked you, Manoel. I wish you could have met her."

"I would have liked that too."

Martin looked back to the forming bust.

"Come on, let's get back to work."

They moved back to the towering figure, trapped in its network of scaffolding.

"Now what kind of reviews will we get for this?" asked the sculptor as he climbed up. "That bloated old queen Peter Bailey probably won't like it at all, but I bet I'll get good reviews from him. He wouldn't write a bad thing about me. I'm his boy!"

"Isn't Peter Bailey the art critic who most supports your work? I remember Ms. Quadras showing me some of his reviews from *The Times*."

"Oh that's sweet Peter all right. Honey drips from his typewriter whenever he writes about me."

"Then why don't you like him? Because he's homosexual?"

"Oh, I don't dislike most homos more than I dislike everybody else. Vicki's a dyke, and I think she's great. But that fat old fool really irritates me."

"Why?" asked the confused priest. "If the man writes well of you, you should appreciate him, unless it's because you think he's stupid for liking what you know to be ridiculous."

"Oh, he's stupid, Manoel. There's no doubt about that. He's a big, fat, slobbering moron, but that's not why I hate him."

"Then why?"

"Remember that I told you I'm a whore?"

The priest nodded.

"Well, Peter Bailey was one of my first tricks. He gave me my first real break by writing me nice reviews, but he didn't write them for free—I can tell you that. After Sharon left, there was nothing I wouldn't do for money and fame, and dear old Peter brought me lots of both."

"I see..."

"Not a very nice thing, is it?"

"No, maybe not, but not much different than the rest of what you told me." The priest moved to the worktable, where he picked up a piece of clay. He molded it into a ball.

"Aren't you offended? Isn't that against your code?"

"Oh, I don't know, Martin. That stuff happens. You want to consider yourself to be a moral failure to punish yourself for your past, and you go out of your way to do things that you find repugnant—anything to increase your misery and to validate your self-image. That's not so terrible, no worse than anything else you've told me. I grew up in an orphanage full of adolescents and spent three years cloistered in a monastery. Priests aren't immune to sins of the flesh any more than anyone else."

"You mean you've slept with men?" Martin was shocked.

"No," replied the priest, "I'm one of the rare people who've lived as long as I have who has never slept with anybody. I was aware of what some of the other boys were doing and had the opportunity, but as I told you, I wanted to be a priest since I was little. No, the sins of the flesh never held much power over me."

"That's what bugged me so much when I met you. You're just too perfect, too much like Sharon, always expecting more from people than they have in them, expecting them to be like you when they can't be."

"Come now, Martin. I didn't expect anything from you when I met you, other than the fact that someday you would have to account for your life in front of God. But as far as I can see, you're redeeming yourself as we speak. You are doing wonderful work, Martin, work I doubt that anyone else is capable of. And I'm proud of you."

"Don't be. I'm not proud of me. I'm happy with this bust, I guess. Though for some reason, the more I work on it, the less satisfied I become. I don't know why. Maybe I'm just tired. But don't be proud of me. I've committed every sin there is, except murder. Living the life I've led, I haven't met many decent people to remind me of my shortcomings, but now here you come after being born into hardship that I can't even imagine, having struggled for every little thing that I take for granted, devoting your life to help the less fortunate. All I do is laugh at people and take from them."

"Well, you're not laughing now, are you?"

"No, I guess I'm not."

"And you're not taking, are you?"

"A million dollars isn't chump change, Manoel."

"But you're earning it. You're creating a marvelous sculpture."

"Maybe I am. But that still doesn't erase the past or turn me into Mr. Wonderful."

"Stop wallowing in this self-pity and self-torture, Martin. I've been there too. I cloistered myself for three years once because I couldn't stand myself for what I had done and wanted to shelter the world from my evil, but eventually the Lord helped me to see that my life was not yet complete. I had more left to do. He gave me a second chance."

"Come on, Manoel, I can't see you ever doing something rotten like me. I've broken all the rules except one. What could you have done?"

Father Manoel looked up painfully to the sculptor above him. Memories flared from the embers of his tortured conscience, which always smoldered darkly, waiting for night when it could burst into his dreams in wild-fired nightmares. Maybe his example could help his friend break this cycle of self-destruction. He continued living after what he had done. He wanted Martin to have a new start too. He didn't want to tell him what had happened—his throat contracted with the thought. Could he tell Martin? Maybe that was his mission with this man.

"Come on, Father, tell me what you could have done to make you understand a person such as I. What did you do that was so awful?"

As Father Manoel started to speak, his voice cracked, hacking his words into a hoarse whisper, "I destroyed an entire people..."

Chapter Twenty-four

"**Y**OU WHAT?"

"I destroyed an entire people, a tribe of Indians."
Father Manoel shuddered as their plaintive moans echoed through the inescapable jungle that loomed darkly around him, always just a word away.

"I killed a people. I wiped them from the earth. All of them, all gone, nobody left at all..."

"What are you talking about, Manoel?"

"I'll tell you. You should know. You aren't the only one plagued by his mistakes. You must keep living. You must keep trying. I do, though at times, especially at night, I wish I didn't have to."

The sculptor dropped his tools in a bucket and climbed down the scaffold to face his friend.

"What happened, Manoel?"

A wave of sadness rolled across the creases of the careworn priest.

"I try not to think about them much during the day—it interferes with my work—but I do pray for them all, one by one, each by name, the seventy-three souls I sent from this earth, seventy-three innocents, all gone because of me. Then there were the others, the Txukarramãe, who I didn't kill, but who I couldn't save. They are almost all gone too, the clan I knew. Some now live in other clans, but the majority are gone. Those poor people. I didn't mean to hurt them. I had good intentions. I wanted to bring them the word of God. I didn't mean to hurt them. I wanted only good..." Father Manoel stared at the floor and drifted into memory.

Martin took him by the arm and led him to a chair beside the worktable.

"Come on Manoel, have a seat. Look, sorry I asked. If you'd rather not talk about it, that's fine. I shouldn't have pried."

The priest looked at him and smiled sadly. "No that's okay, my son. I want you to hear this. Maybe it will help you to see that you really haven't led such an awful life. Others have done much worse. Let me tell you."

Martin took a seat beside him, and the priest began to talk.

"I wasn't always an educator. I had other interests when I was at seminary—I wanted to be a missionary. I wanted to spread Catholicism to the corners of the world, the world that took from me my mother, sister and the brother I never knew. I wanted to run out of the seminary gates waving the flaming brand of goodness. I wanted to conquer evil. Our church is not very evangelical, not anymore. But in those days, we had our missions, and I wanted one. I was young and full of fire, so I petitioned for an assignment in the Amazon, which I easily won—there weren't many interested takers. It was hard duty, in the heart of our country, far from any of the amenities that most people can't do without. And it was often dangerous. In those days, dozens of tribes had yet to be approached and pacified, and many were very dangerous to men who ventured into their territory. Rubber tappers often vanished, their goods later turning up in Indian camps, and some missionaries disappeared too. Strangers to the uninitiated Indian were considered a threat, which often times they were. Indians in the region weren't cannibals, but they generally killed anyone who wasn't from their tribe, taking from them whatever they had. It was both a way of getting tools and food, and a method of self-preservation.

"I wasn't afraid, though. I was excited. Oh, I was afraid, sure, but wouldn't admit it. I was too young to be honest with myself back then. What little fear I had was overwhelmed by the excitement of finally walking out from the bosom of my mother church and entering the world to pay her back for all that she had given me. I wanted to work, and I was ready to go, so with all of my farewells said, I boarded a bus that took me to Belém, a city at the mouth of the Amazon. There I met the mission director, who gave me advice, supplies and one last final blessing. Then he helped me board a riverboat, and I was on my way.

"We headed up the river, so wide that you couldn't see its banks for over a day, and then made our turn south into the Rio Xingu. The trip upstream to its headwaters took over a week of constant steaming, until the end at least, when they only navigated during the day for fear of grounding. Martin, you can't imagine those rivers. The Amazon seems like a muddy sea when you're on it, not like a river at all, and the Xingu, though much smaller, is at its mouth immense. You have the feeling that the world is water, brown water bounded by trees so distant that they appear to be nothing more than an endless thin ribbon, a slender green horizon.

"I remember that trip well. I would stare out across the water and into the distance, wondering what lay beyond the green, wondering if I had what it took to be a good missionary, and wondering if I would encounter danger in these primitive people that I sought—wondering more and more about it as we moved up the narrowing river and into the expanding world of trees. As we neared our destination, a government camp called Capitão Vasconcelos, the river narrowed greatly and it seemed as if the current increased. What was once a placid field of brown punctuated on occasion by a jumping fish or the dive of a fisher hawk, became agitated with ripples from the current beneath its surface. And as the banks grew closer, we could hear the constant calls of birds and monkeys howling in the trees. Twice at night we were awoken by the huffing roar of a jaguar."

"I think if I were you at that point, I would have had them turn the boat around," said Martin. "Jesus, Manoel, you were right out there in a jungle full of jaguars."

"Oh yes. And in that part of the forest, far from any settlement, they had no fear of man. Jaguars, anacondas, alligators, piranhas—it was quite an adventure for a young man who had spent his life in an orphanage and then seminary."

"You're crazy. I would have been scared to death."

"No, it was exciting! Maybe if I had been a little older, I would have had more fear—you can't imagine what it's like to be startled awake by one of those big cats—but I think that the only thing that really bothered me then was a rising doubt in my ability to carry out my mission. I was so young, I wondered if anyone would take me seriously. The rubber tappers and Indians who journeyed with us until São Felix didn't seem impressed, and the captain and his crew of one, Jorge, would never stop laughing—I thought the joke might have been me. And the other Indian, a Juruna, who was returning with me from a government hospital in Belém back to Capitão Vasconcelos, well, he said nothing at all. He just sat under the canopy and stared out into the trees.

"After nine days on the river, we finally made the camp, which was nothing more than a few scattered huts, a

197

mandioca planting and an airstrip hacked out of the jungle near the bank of the river. We tied up to a tree and jumped ashore. I was in the jungle for the next two years."

He mused on that time as he sat with the sculptor and silently drifted back into the black waters of his memory:

"What have you brought for us today, your wives and mothers?" asked the grizzled and bearded man who looked over sixty, but who turned out later to be the head of the camp—and only thirty-five.

"No, something even better, João," replied the captain with a grin. "We brought you a priest and another Indian!"

"They all hooted and carried on as if it was the funniest thing they had ever heard. Even the Indian, who I had begun to think mute, joined in and whooped himself into a ball upon the ground, kicking up a cloud of dust to the amusement of the others, who laughed even louder. The hilarity spread like a debilitating fever, striking its victims with side-splitting seizures that seemed to threaten to burst them apart, and I was the only one not infected. Finally, the fever broke into scattered gasps heaved from sore ribs, and introductions were made. I soon found that diversions were few in the jungle and that insane laughter at anything, punctuated by long periods of brooding silence and stories told over and over again, were the only after-hours entertainment to be had. The three men in camp were *Nordestino caboclos* like me, men of mixed race from the dry Sertão in the northeast. They must have been running from something or somebody to have ended up at Capitão Vasconcelos, but I was wise enough not to ask.

"They were a rough bunch, half-naked and as brown as any Indian, with a look in their eyes that made one think twice, but they were nice enough. I was a great friend to all because I had thought to bring some old newspapers with month-old *futebol* scores, and from then on, I was always welcome in their camp. After several months in the jungle, I understood their laughter and was, at times, as hysterical as anybody.

"I left the next day with the Indian I had traveled down with, a Juruna named Samiri, now a friend through laughter. Once the men at the camp accepted me, he did too, so off we went, he taking me to the village of my mission three weeks distant from his own. Indians are like that. Time and distance don't matter.

"The trip downriver in a dugout with Samiri was my introduction to the ways of the Indians. His life was hours of silence, blending into the river and the forest around us as he paddled, bow-fished or hunted, broken only at strange intervals by short strings of incomprehensible language and pantomime. A day would pass in which he said nothing; he was a concentrated master of his realm. Then moved by some imperceptible mental click, he would drop whatever he was doing and his eyes would twinkle with the joke that shook him, which he tried to convey to me with flailing arms and strange words shot rapid-fire from the gaping grin ensconced above his lip disk. Then with another click, he was again the stoic warrior. Lord of the jungle and happy infant in one, he was typical of the people I had come to save for God. Our friendship grew with the passing river, until in darkness, he delivered me to the footpath that would take me to my village. He could not come with me because the tribes were not friendly. With a handshake, he was gone, paddling quickly away. I never saw him again.

"I spent that night sleepless, camped by the river's edge. Then with first light, I headed down the trail to a reception I hoped would be friendly."

"You mean you didn't know how they would receive you?" asked the sculptor, amazed.

"No, not really. Members of the Central Brazilian Foundation had made contact with the Txukarramãe the previous year during an expedition to map the geographical center of Brazil. The contact had been peaceful, and the expedition leader had promised that he would send a missionary in return for the two warriors he took with him. It was sort of a cultural exchange. The primary goal of the Central Brazilian Foundation was to pave the way for development in the region, and the expedition leader, Orlando Villas Boas, thought the only chance that fragile Indian cultures had to survive the coming onslaught of civilization was by the gradual introduction of our modern ways, which he knew would overwhelm them if the Indians were confronted head on. It's very hard for a Stone Age man to adapt to modern thought.

"A king of the jungle can lose his feathered crown when attacked with guns instead of arrows, or with trade or electricity. He can easily lose his place in the world and then his desire for living. A frustrated Indian deprived of his role as a hunter and warrior often gives up on life, lies down and dies. Villas Boas wanted to save them from that fate by slowly letting them become aware of us and the world that was beginning to push toward them from the edges of the forest. This tribe was known to have killed many rubber tappers, and Villas Boas knew that they couldn't continue, or eventually the *seringueiros* would mass and seek vengeance. Rubber was a valuable commodity in a poor country. Men were seeking it, and more men would follow. My job was to civilize the Indians enough so that they would no longer kill on sight every non-tribal member they encountered on their lands. So, there I was marching into a camp of warriors on a promise of safe passage over nine months old. It was a bit nerve-wracking, but all went well.

"At the end of trail, I held up my hands in a gesture of friendship and shouted out a loud 'hello,' which had me surrounded by some very angry warriors who then poked and prodded me across the village to the glowering chief, who like the rest of them, was baffled by my intrusion. At first he was grimacing and wary, but at the mention of Villas Boas and the names of the Txukarramãe he took with him, I was immediately accepted as a friend. I stayed with them two years, and in that time, I learned their language and taught them as much as I could about us, our religion and the world that was rolling relentlessly toward them. I wasn't teaching really, just building friendship more than anything. Most of what I said was nodded at, hooted at and then discarded as undecipherable nonsense. But still, we were friends, and that was enough. I hoped that friendship would be their salvation. It was not.

"It was often my habit to canoe a day downstream and spend time with a Lutheran missionary, Barry Blackwell, who ministered to another clan of the Txukarramãe. He is the man who now runs the Lutheran Seafarer's House where I'm staying. He arrived in the Xingu soon after I did, and even through language difficulties and religious differences, we became fast friends. I had spent a fortnight with him that final time and then hurried back to my tribe. Guilt had been building for neglecting them so long, and it was well justified. I returned to a celebration, a victory dance. The tribe was singing and dancing, but the festivities hushed as soon as I entered camp.

"Everyone dispersed, avoiding my eyes as they took shelter in their banana leaf lean-tos. I soon discovered what victory had taken place—the village was littered with the tools of *seringueiros*, and the bones of a cooked mule. All of my lecturing had been for nothing. They had murdered more Brazilians. I confronted the chief and warned him of its consequences, future retribution by bands of armed men, but he either wouldn't or couldn't comprehend. All was forgotten by everyone but me, who kept preaching peace and a changing world.

"Well, the world did change…two weeks later when a band of *seringueiros* came in the night and attacked our sleeping village with rifles. I reacted immediately and ran out to stand before the village, shouting in Portuguese for the shooting to stop. The panicked Indians flocked to me and huddled around me, frightened by the noise and the flash of death raining from the rifles, hugging their wounded and screaming out into the sounding darkness. The gunfire died down as the *seringueiros* circled slowly in upon us. Their leader broke from their midst and walked to me, silent but with vengeance in his eyes. I identified myself and beseeched him to kill no more and to leave the village. His revenge had been won, and I promised that the Indians wouldn't retaliate. How could they? They were only armed with bows and arrows and crude stone knives. He stared at me a moment—I can still see his malice licked up by the firelight—and then for an answer, he shot me in the chest."

"They shot you!" exclaimed the sculptor, appalled.

"Yes, twice in the chest. I only remember the first shot, but I woke up delirious three months later in a hospital in Belém with two wounds that were just beginning to heal because of an infection I contracted in the jungle."

"How did you get out?"

"Apparently the survivors of the attack drug the wounded to the river and paddled us to the other clan downstream. From there, Barry Blackwell took us down to Capitão Vasconcelos, which had medical supplies. I was then airlifted to Belém by the Air Force."

"What happened to the Indians?"

"I didn't know until five months later. Barry had been relieved of his mission and was returning home. He sought me out before he left and told me what had happened: twenty Txukarramãe died the night I was shot, and another fifteen died later of their wounds. Since most of the dead were warriors, the providers of food, the tribe could no longer function on its own, so it was absorbed into the other clan. Of the wounded, ten recovered, leaving a total of forty Indians, mostly women and children. Barry's village was also attacked two years later and most of the survivors from my clan were killed then."

"That's awful, Manoel. But surely you don't hold yourself responsible for their deaths? You can't possibly. What happened to them was what you were trying to prevent."

"Oh, I'll always feel responsible for them. If I hadn't left my village to visit my friend, I might have been able to prevent them from killing the *seringueiros*. I'll never know about that. But I didn't lose my faith because of the Txukarramãe. In fact, I went back to the Xingu after my wounds healed, a year later. I wanted to put the lessons I had learned into practice in order to protect other, more remote Indians from the fate that befell the Txukarramãe.

"It had been a rough year for me, lying in bed with nothing else to think of, other than the fate of the Indians I had lived with and taught. I was very sick too. One of the bullets I took punctured a lung that became infected, so I was plagued by pneumonia and flu the entire time I was in the hospital. Sickness, though, couldn't stop me. As soon as I could get up and walk, I petitioned for another mission and, weak or not, I was soon steaming down the Xingu in hopes of succeeding where I had once failed."

"You went back after having been shot?" asked Martin, incredulously.

"Of course. I was a missionary, and I had work to do. I went back to Capitão Vasconcelos and asked to be sent where I was needed. If the men in camp seemed surprised to see me again, none of them let on. The jungle is full of surprises, and as I said before, no one asks questions, especially if he wishes to guard his own past and retain his own anonymity. I was back. That's all.

"At that time, all of the pacified tribes had contact with missionaries and didn't have a great need of me, but there were other tribes that were known to exist through conversations with other Indians and sightings of their village smoke by the Air Force. One of these tribes, the Suyá, was believed to be relatively close to Capitão Vasconcelos, a week downriver between camp and my former village. I volunteered to make contact. With a shrug, João, the camp leader, accepted my offer and explained to me the methods used to make first contact with an unknown tribe. He also gave me the supplies and trinkets needed for the task. Then, with one of my former parishioners acting as my guide—a surviving Txukarramãe who had walked into camp a few days before—I was in a canoe and paddling north. After a week of paddling, we reached the mouth of one of the Xingu's tributaries, the Suyá-Missu, which we entered and then headed east. A few days of searching revealed a trail that led from the river into suspected Suyá territory. There, my guide and I split company. He couldn't stay with me, because the Txukarramãe had raided the Suyá twenty years before, and his presence would have probably been a death sentence for both of us. Though it was right for him to leave,

I still watched him paddle away with deep regret. I was alone in hostile territory, unarmed.

"Following João's instructions, I laid out presents—fishing hooks and line, and knives and beads—and then left for safer ground across the river. I went a kilometer inland, where I camped hidden and without a fire for a few days. They were long days, believe me. It was hard. I was still sick with the last round of flu I caught in the hospital. I was feverish, miserable and scared. I feared for my life. These first encounters with Indians are always touch-and-go, and I could have easily been tracked down and murdered for the goods I was offering. But what I feared most was that my mission would come to nothing as it had with the Txukarramãe. I wanted to ready these people for the coming onslaught of civilization. I needed to save their earthly lives before I could save their souls.

"Three days after I had left them, I checked the gifts that I had set out across the river. They were gone, and in their place were the tracks of several men that led back up the trail. It was a good sign. My gifts had been accepted, and it didn't seem as if anyone was tracking me. I laid out more, then returned across river to sweat it out again. Three days later, these gifts were gone as well. One final time, I laid out my bait and then returned to my camp to wait and sweat and pray. And pray and pray and pray.

"Three days passed before I presented my last and final offering, which included me. I camped beside my gifts and prayed not to be a sacrifice to futility. That night the Suyá came. I was awoken with a rough kick and found myself surrounded by mean-faced, painted warriors with bows pulled taught and poison arrows at the ready, all pointed at me. I greeted them in a language common with several other tribes in the region and asked to be taken to their chief so that I could offer him further gifts of peace. Without a word, my request was granted, and I was hurried down the darkened trail by the silent warriors, some of whom were sporting the beads I had earlier set out.

"The Suyá camp was different than that of the Txukarramãe. They lived communally in thatched long houses, while the Txukarramãe lived in primitive lean-tos. They were more advanced and less aggressive. I explained to the chief that I had come in friendship, and he, on examining the gifts I brought, accepted me as a guest. It would have been better for them all if they had killed me at the water's edge and thrown me in the river."

"Why do you say that?" questioned Martin, who had been listening to the story as intently as he would to any tale of fiction beyond the scope of his life.

"Why? I'll tell you why. I was sick, Martin. I brought flu into the tribe. Our diseases aren't natural to the Amazon. They had no immunities. Those poor people didn't have a chance. Where those rubbers tappers who attacked my other tribe had failed with guns, I succeeded with an outstretched hand and smiling lips touched to a communal calabash. People started dying before I'd been there a week. I did all I could to aid them. I had a simple kit of drugs I'd brought from Capitão Vasconcelos, but it was nothing to stem the creeping tide of death that washed over us. Twelve were dead in two weeks, and most of the others were down with fever. When I was out of medicine, I did the only thing left for me to do—taking two of the last healthy warriors, I left and paddled back to the government camp for more supplies and for the help of anyone more useful than myself. By paddling hard we made it upriver in a week, but not without cost: one of my warriors got sick and died along the way.

"When we returned two weeks later with João and all the medicine he had, we returned to nothing. Everyone was dead. Some were buried, but most were splayed out wherever they laid down to take their final breath. Seventy-two souls gone, and the last was on his way. The warrior, Megliruini, who paddled with me tirelessly to bring more medicine to his people, simply gave up when he found his family gone. He wanted to join them, so he laid down in the middle of camp, stared up to the canopy and answered their call. While João and I worked to bury the dead, he worked to become one. He was the last we buried."

Father Manoel's eyes teared at the thought of Megliruini, the last of a brave people who had managed to survive all the dangers of the jungle except the open hand of a priest—a Judas hand, the hand of death. He looked up from the workbench to the incredulous eyes of the stunned and silent sculptor.

"So you see, Martin. You aren't alone in your mistakes. Others have done worse, much worse. Believe me. I was like you were for a long time. When I left the jungle, I cloistered myself in a monastery. I wanted to lock myself away to prevent myself from wreaking any further wrong. I spent three years, silent, lost in constant prayer to a God who I wasn't sure existed anymore, praying for the souls entrusted in my care who I destroyed, and praying that he would never allow me to be a vessel of evil again. How I despaired. I think if I had been as strong as Megliruini, I would have been able to give up and die. I wanted to, and gave up all hope, but somehow, I kept on living.

"Slowly, after a year or so, I entered into the work routine of the monastery. The brothers were a self-sustaining order. They tilled their own fields and baked their own bread, and with their excess bounty, they provided for an orphanage attached to the order a few kilometers distant in the city. One day, after two more years had passed, when I had integrated well enough into the daily routine, I was ordered to deliver lunch to the orphans, so with the help of a brother, I loaded our van and drove into town.

"It was quite a shock for me to pass beyond the monastery walls. I was unnerved by the noise of passing cars and trucks, and by the glances of passers-by who I knew could read the crimes forever printed on my face. I was then so different than the rash young man who journeyed alone into the jungle. I wanted to run back to the monastic sanctuary, but knew I couldn't until our work was done. Silently, I drove on.

"We were greeted at the orphanage gate by a smiling nun and by the laughter of children. They were everywhere, playing *futebol,* running, jumping, all full of the spirit and the joy of life. It took me back to my days as an orphan. I thought of all of the kids I had grown up with and wondered what became of them. I was one of the lucky ones who was educated and had a future. The rest, I knew, were probably back on the streets we had come from, jobless and without hope or opportunity to escape the poverty we were born into. It was then, watching those smiling, happy children, that I realized I still had value. I could be an educator and could give kids a chance to succeed in life. I could give them a chance to keep smiling. When we returned, I informed the abbot that I was ready to leave and knew that my calling was education. These were the first words I had spoken in years, and they felt good rolling from my mouth. The abbot gave me his blessing and sent me to the orphanage school the next day. I've been teaching now for over twenty years."

Martin had been paralyzed with the gravity of the priest's tragic past, but when the conversation moved to Father Manoel's current work, it was once more safe ground.

"That's great, Manoel. I'm glad that you've managed to put it all behind you."

"I have. I'm at peace now, most of the time. Nightmares haunt me still, and I get sad when I remember. But I'm at peace. I will always feel responsible for what happened, Martin, but there is a greater will and a higher understanding. I trust in God. I found him again through children and understand that his world is too complex for us, that it defies our understanding. It is enough to know that he wants us to do good in life.

"Now, with your help, I will be able to. I started this nursery and educational program eleven years ago, and now because of you, our first graduates will be able to walk down the aisle and into better lives. You and your work are now a part of that."

"Well, I hope you like this when it's finished, but I don't know if I'm as excited about this bust as I was when we started." Martin looked up doubtfully to the giant above him, now almost complete.

"Don't be silly, Martin. It will be a masterpiece."

"Well, we'll see about that once it's cast and ready. I'm not so sure."

"You know, Martin, I don't believe you would have cared one way or the other a month ago when I met you."

"I probably wouldn't have, Manoel. I probably wouldn't have. But I'd better do this one right, or I'll never get rid of you. And I want to pack you up and send you back to Brazil with your bag of money as soon as possible. You've got work to do down there. And, I have work to do here. I'd better get going or I'll be up all night. I have an appointment with the plaster caster early tomorrow. After that, you and I will make a trip to Queens to the foundry. Think about it, Manoel. In just a little while, you'll have your statue."

"I can't wait, Martin. It's the answer to my prayers."

"I hope so. Now, back to work."

The sculptor spidered up his scaffold and began to work where he'd left off. He picked up one of the last pieces of the puzzle and deftly stitched it in.

"Martin?" said Father Manoel. He was preparing to repeat a question, but this time he hoped for a positive answer.

"Yeah," replied the sculptor, who didn't look down.

"Since you are doing work like this now, are you going to go back to selling Vicki's work under your name? You could become famous for this type of sculpture. Maybe your time as a junkman has passed. Maybe you've made your point. We know how tasteless some people can be. Now go out and find those with taste. They're out there, and you know it."

"I'll think about it, Manoel."

"Good... *Meu Deus!* It's three o'clock. I've got to get back to the UN before they close. I'll call you tomorrow. Good luck with your work, *amigo.*"

"Thanks, Manoel. Good luck with your paperwork. And thanks for sharing your story. You've helped me a lot, Father."

"I'm glad, my son. I hoped to."

The sculptor watched the priest leave, thinking about what he'd said. Father Manoel was right. It was time for him to forget and move on. If the priest had managed to sort out his awful life, then maybe he could too. His past seemed trivial in comparison. He should quit this racket and do good work. Money wasn't a problem. What was? With his reputation, he could sell anything—good sculpture as well as bad. He could turn himself around, and then at the end of his career, he might leave the world a lasting legacy for which he would be remembered. Well, it was something to strive for, anyway. Time was the judge of true greatness.

Time would tell. Father Manoel was right. Martin knew what he needed to do.

An electricity filled him, which he hadn't felt since college when he used to lay his head in Sharon's lap, look up to her and tell her that he would make it one day, that he would be an artist who was remembered. She believed him then, and he could make her believe again. She would know if he turned around. She must still keep current in art, knowing her. She'd be happy if he changed. He wanted that for her, but mostly he wanted it for himself.

He swung down from the scaffold and landed lightly on his feet. Then he jogged to the living room where he plugged in the phone and punched in a number.

"Yeah?"

"Vicki, it's Martin."

"Oh, hi..." Her usually abrasive questioning deflated to sullen squawk. "Look, if you're calling about those mannequins, forget about it. I already told Armine that I need another week. There are only three of us down here now, for Christ's sake. If you need them that bad, why don't you come down and lend a hand. A little work never killed anybody."

"I didn't call about the mannequins, Vicki."

"Then what do you want? We're busy here. I don't have time to waste on the phone."

"Vicki, I wanted to apologize."

"Apologize?"

"That's right, about the way I treated you the other day. I'm sorry, Vicki, and I want to make it up. Remember the raise you wanted?"

"Sure, I remember. Twenty-five percent. Big deal. What do you want? A hand job? Am I supposed to bark like a dog and roll over?"

"No, Vicki. I know hand jobs aren't your style. Listen, I'm doubling your pay, retroactive to when you asked for it."

"No joke?"

"No joke."

"Geez boss, sounds like you just got a hand job. Why the change of heart?"

"Well, little Vick, I guess that even a prick needs a couple of friends in the world, and you've always been a good one. Besides, you deserve the money."

"Glad you're starting to realize that." Her voice was softening with every passing syllable.

"Vicki, there's more. I've got some ideas of my own that I want to work on..."

"Damn, Martin, your liver giving out? You don't sound so good."

"My liver's feeling better by the day, and once I'm through with this commission, I want to help you with your own showing."

"My own showing? Do you mean it, Martin?"

"I mean it Vick. You've earned it, and I think I'll be going my own direction from now on."

"Thanks, boss! I don't know what to say," she said, her voice full of emotion.

"Say goodbye, Vicki. I've got to get back to work. Pop over some night for a visit. Bye." Martin hung up, happy. Then he turned back to his work. It loomed majestic before him. But in all its majesty, he still didn't know. *Was this God?* He shrugged away the thought. He didn't have time for it. The casters were coming in the morning, and there was still much left to do.

Chapter Twenty-five

FATHER MANOEL HESITATED AT the door. The winter's cold pushed him in, yet he resisted, wary of the hellish scene before him. Heavyset and sooty men hammered, struggled and shouted through labors he didn't understand, and waves of white heat rolled from a roaring furnace at the other end of the cavernous maw. No treble-headed guard dog blocked his path. The space was his to enter. He tentatively stepped over the threshold and wandered through the mayhem, searching for his friend.

"Manoel! Manoel! Up here!"

He looked up to see Martin beckoning down from a catwalk strung high along a blackened wall.

"Come up here." The sculptor motioned to the metal stair that led up to his thin and doubtful perch. The priest tapped up it quickly, glad to have an assigned place away from the bedlam below.

"Did you have trouble getting here?"

"No, I took the subway to Flushing Station and caught a cab from there—just like you told me. It was fast."

"Good.

"Sorry I couldn't come to get you, but I've been here all night lining this up. I'll drop you off when we're done. How was Washington?"

"A waste of time. I went all the way down there just to find out that I have to apply for U.S. Aide grants through the American embassy in Brasília. If they had told me that on the phone when I first inquired, I wouldn't have made the trip in the first place."

"You've got to be kidding, you mean you went down there for nothing?"

"That's right."

"I can't believe it. Sorry to hear it."

"It's all right. I'm used to dealing with government. But traveling around is expensive, and I can't afford trips like that. How was your week?"

"Good. I've been working nights with these guys to get this ready. The foundry couldn't fit us in during regular hours for another three weeks, but I have two half-crews working for me on overtime. We work from six to ten at night and then from four to eight in the morning. It was hard to figure out how exactly to cast this: the bust is complicated because it's made of so many freestanding pieces. I was afraid we were going to have to cast them all individually and weld them on the armature one by one. But Jimmy, the foreman, is very good and he found a way to cast the entire bust at once. The set-up was complicated, but when it's cast, there won't be any real work left, other than simple things like chasing out the seams left by the mold and installing the lighting, and maybe filling in an odd pore. These guys can do the finish work in hours. So tonight, you'll meet your maker, Manoel—if all goes right. I don't know about this concept of God. I hope it's what we're looking for."

"Of course it is, Martin. This statue is the most wonderful thing I've ever seen. I can't wait to see it finished. So, what is it you want to show me at five in the morning?"

The sculptor's eyes were animated. "The casting, Manoel. We're going to cast this morning. Everything's set, but I had the guys wait until you got here. I love this part. Most sculptors don't even show up for it, but for me, it's something special. The birth of a statue! Its creation. And I thought maybe you'd like to be here for it—since he's yours."

"Thanks, Martin. I'm glad I came. I'm excited."

The priest and sculptor grinned at each other like young boys awaiting their father's okay to burst through the door and attack the presents around the tree on Christmas morning. Martin turned and shouted down to the floor, "Ready, Jimmy!"

The foreman jerked a thumb in acknowledgment, then limped over to the furnace. He was a powerful man, but misshapen. His biceps bulged like barreled hams, and his arms were thick with deltas of veins rushing with the headwaters coursing down from his immense chest and shoulders. But when he moved, he pushed ahead graceless, like a fullback mowing through the line, trying to shake off a dragging tackle from his thin and damaged leg. And the face beneath his close-cut curls was pocked by slag or disease. But ugly or not, to the furnaces and the men about him, he was the undisputed lord and master of their craft.

He stopped before the furnace and checked its draft by eye.

"Metal hot, Fred?" he asked, though he knew the answer.

Fred double-checked the thermometer on the panel and responded above the roar, "Yeah, Jimmy!"

Jimmy nodded and faced the others. "Let's go, boys!"

Two big men tugged a huge iron pitcher suspended by an enormous chainfall that hung from a car on a monorail track bedded in the ceiling girders. Upon reaching the furnace front, they spun chains in a clattered whirl, and slowly the pitcher descended. When it reached level with a spigot at the furnace bottom, Jimmy checked the pitcher's position. Not satisfied, he signaled with a finger for his men to inch it closer. They stopped when he raised a muscled fist.

"Stand clear!"

They all moved back at his command. Then when all were at a safe distance, he looked to Fred, who was now clad in a heavy apron, asbestos gloves and a face shield.

Jimmy roared, "Fire in the bucket!" And Fred struck open a sluice with a ten-pound sledge.

Molten metal erupted from the blast furnace in a volcanic river of heat and light that frothed into the pitcher, billowing smoke and turning it a dull red. When the flood had ended, the men began to pull the pitcher quickly to the mold. At its base they strained at their chains, hoisting the bucket slowly above them. When it reached its zenith above the mold, Jimmy shouted, "Hold it! Now inch her over. More. More. More. Stop!"

He motioned the other men away. Then he took the chain of the tipping arm and with measured strength, he expertly directed a flow of bronze into the hissing mold.

The sculptor and the priest watched the burning liquor pour from the crucible into the mound below it, mesmerized by the power of the scene and their desire. Blood into stone. Life into clay. Creation poured in a rain of fired gold, and they both prayed for its deliverance. The face of God, unveiled! This was their heartfelt plea.

With the last drop gone and the pitcher empty, Jimmy released his chain and motioned his men to move the rig away. He limped slowly around the mold, touching it lightly with callused fingers, feeling for even heat. Satisfied, he faced the men above him and thrust up a thumb in triumph.

"It's a clean cast, Mr. Drake! We'll have her broken out and set up tonight, all chased out with the light installed and everything, just like you asked."

"Thanks, Jimmy." Martin smiled and waved down his appreciation, then he patted his friend on the shoulder. "Let's go home, Manoel. I need to get some sleep."

Chapter Twenty-six

⟫⟩⟩⟩⟩⟩——————⟨⟨⟨⟨

T HE NIGHTTIME TRAFFIC ON Northern Boulevard was
as brisk as ever. What had once been the farm road
that led F. Scott Fitzgerald and Jay Gatsby out through hay
fields to East and West Egg had become a major thoroughfare
of an expanded city. It was Italian where they caught it at
the foot of the Queensborough bridge that spanned the East
River from Midtown Manhattan, but the line of pizza joints
that first rolled by them was gradually being culled and
replaced by clovered neon signs pledging dark stout beer and
tragic songs strung from drunken fiddles in teary Irish lilts.

Their destination was close at hand, a foundry on
Flushing Bay ensconced between La Guardia and Flushing
Meadows, where the Mets cracked homers and where tennis
balls jetted back and forth during the annual magic of the
U.S. Open. Just a few miles north, through a galaxy of traffic
lights, the boulevard would again transform, abandoning
leprechaun green for the color of money . The world of Jay
Gatsby lived on in mansions set on pampered lawns that
rolled out to taste the expensive salt lapping up from Long
Island sound. Gatsby's jaded legacy sparkled brighter than
before in its gaudy, hopeless bounty. But their journey didn't
take them there. They sought industry, the soiled manger of
creation, and that day, it awaited them in Flushing.

As Martin drew to a stop at yet another traffic light, Father Manoel continued in his excitement, "Martin, I just can't wait to see your statue, bigger than life in bronze!"

"I know, you just said that."

He put his Porsche in gear and idled ahead slowly, following the parade of cars before them.

"I know I'm talking too much, but I just can't help it. All your work is about to pay off, and all of my prayers will be answered."

"Hold all that until we see it."

"Come on, Martin. You've done it! You saved my crèches and created your magnum opus. Where's your faith?"

The sculptor brooded through his windshield at the taillights close ahead and wondered. He had fought himself for a week to come up with this concept, then battled several days to fix it in clay, and now? Now what?

He had worked night and day for over a month, expanding his model, painstakingly fostering its growth from poor beginnings as humble earth into what he hoped would be his masterwork. But was he elated? Was he excited? No. He was filled with doubt and dread. Something wasn't right.

Where was the hand of the god that Father Manoel had served for a lifetime? Where was the god that Father Manoel spent hours droning on about in his studio? It didn't feel right. Martin didn't feel inspired. He felt foreboding. What he needed now was silence to sort through this agitation. Maybe it was just nerves. He hadn't had much sleep since he started this project. *Yes, that was probably all he needed, just a little peace and quiet*, Martin thought. But he wasn't going to get any now, not with Father Manoel blurting out his enthusiasm at every passing block.

Martin mulled silently through his doubt and his growing aggravation with his happy friend as they drove the last mile and then turned left onto a road that led east to an industrial park that housed the foundry. It was a collection of ugly, damaged shells strung out along the shores of the sullied, dirty bay. He made good time up the less traveled byway and managed to gear up to fourth for the first time since he left his apartment. Just as they reached the foundry entrance, Martin cut close around a limousine, which to his surprise, followed them into the parking lot and drew to a stop beside them. They were climbing out of his sports car just as Harry Banks was being ushered from the limo by his taut chauffeur.

"Drake, you should be an Indy driver or a Mexican cabby! You gave Edmund here quite a start out there on the road."

"Sorry," said the sculptor, disconcerted by his gaffe and by the presence of the billionaire.

The chauffeur answered, "It was nothing, sir, nothing at all."

"Good evening, Father Manoel." Banks stepped over and shook the hand of the smiling priest.

"Hello, Harry. I'm surprised to see you. I didn't think that you could come."

"I did have a meeting tonight, but your enthusiasm on the phone got me thinking that this must be something I wouldn't want to miss."

He turned to Martin and held out his hand. They shook firmly. There was a glimmer in the old man's eye as he sized him up anew.

"Mr. Drake, Father Manoel thinks you're the new Da Vinci, and that was enough of a shock to get me down here. I don't like missing miracles when they come, since they are so rare and since I won't be around to see many more. Please tell me, what have you done that's so enthralled the Father?"

"I don't know, tried to fulfill our contract, I guess."

"Well, let's have a look at your work."

The billionaire pushed through the door, followed first by the priest and finally by the hesitant and sullen sculptor—who wished they would both just disappear.

They entered into darkness, broken only by the dull light pouring from the smudged panes of Jimmy's office windows across the floor.

"Hey Jimmy! Can we get some light on in here?" Martin shouted across the void. He was answered by two flashlight beams, which shot out of the office and then played along the floor, sweeping toward them. A click, click, click of heels identified Armine, and there was a strange sliding gait that could only have been Jimmy.

"Armine?"

"Hi, sweet cheeks."

"What are you doing here?"

"Do you think I'd miss a chance of seeing this thing that's kept you out of commission so long? I'm going to have it boxed up tonight and delivered to that..."

She switched gears as she neared, recognizing the men who stood with Martin, and said quickly, "Why Mr. Banks! How good of you to come!"

Sugar filled the air as she clicked over faster to greet him.

"And Father Manoel, what a nice surprise!"

She was good for at least an hour of inanities, but Martin, impatient, stole the stage. "What's the matter, Jimmy? Power out?"

"No, Mr. Drake. I cut the lights so you could see it in the dark first."

"Everyone's in showbiz," grumbled the sculptor.

Jimmy let it pass. He was thinking of the statue.

"Just wait until you see it. Please everyone, this way."

Jimmy guided them to a spot ten feet distant from the base of the bust.

"Get ready everyone!" Jimmy said. He limped behind the hulking sculpture where his light gave a dim outline to its form and dimension. A switch snapped, but nothing happened.

Jimmy cursed quietly to himself then spoke to the others.

"Sorry, Folks. The breaker must be off. Hang on."

He pushed off through the darkness, foot dragging as he went.

"Gentlemen, if I may," cooed Armine. "I need to borrow my artist for a moment. He's been working so hard on your statue that we've fallen out of touch."

She took Martin by the arm and towed him away from the others, out of whisper distance.

"Martin, I've been trying to get hold of you for over two weeks. Why did you disconnect your phone?"

"I didn't want interruptions. What's up?"

"Why did you bring Banks here?"

"I didn't. Manoel did. I don't want him here."

"Me neither. This would have played better in the gallery with champagne and lighting, maybe an organ— church music. Well, we'll just have to make the best of it.

"Look, be ready in case Banks likes this. If he's taken with it, let's lean on him to get his wallet out and commission another one while it's still hot on his mind. Just think of all of those poor sweet children in Brazil."

She smiled, and in the torchlight she looked ghoulish.

Martin looked at her and wondered why he had ever liked her. He said nothing.

"I also need to talk to you about Vicki..."

"That's something I want to discuss too, Armine. I've talked it over with Vick, and I've agreed to help her with a solo exhibition."

"You what?" Armine shouted.

It echoed through the foundry like an harpy shriek in a box canyon . Armine caught herself and hissed more softly, "Are you crazy? We can't do that. Plastic surgery couldn't make her photogenic, and once she opens her mouth—forget it. She'll chase out customers faster than I could draw them in. She couldn't sell a nuke wholesale to Saddam Hussein. Put that to rest and be realistic. She stays in the factory. Oh, and that giant pay raise you gave her was a huge mistake. She'll just keep nibbling at you and wheedling for more. She needed a pay raise, but double her salary? You're crazy. There was no need for it. I don't know what's gotten into you lately, Martin. I think that all the hours you've put into this have addled you. Forget about Vicki. I'll handle her if you can't."

"Armine. We're doing it. I gave her my word."

"Forget it."

Martin was about to argue when Jimmy shouted, "Everybody ready?"

They returned to stand with the others.

"Go ahead, Jimmy," said Martin, though he didn't really want him to.

With the touch of a switch the foundry came alive with light and beauty, for centered on its floor was a visage with a splendor and power never pictured by man. God rose above them, shoulders drawing up from the earth in an image of his glory that was, for an instant, intelligible—an image of the creator bound by the terms of his creation.

The magic broke with the flash of light. This creator of man as cast in their image was not the creator at all, he was within that façade, beaming through its bronze constraints, threatening to sunder them with energy beyond belief or understanding. Light beamed down to them in streams cast from pitying eyes and rifts in metal fabric. Silly are you humans, it seemed to say, for trying to picture that beyond you. Pitiful, inadequate and lost, my children, seek your Father in his house not in futile temples. Carve me in your hearts and not in stone.

But even as he spread beyond dimension in a shattering of light, the sculpture somehow held—a snapshot of a failed attempt to attain that which was beyond conception.

All stood still, awed by the power in the bronze, daring not to break the silence of the sculptor with inadequate words of praise that could only fall at his feet, unworthy of hearing.

Finally, Armine spoke into the tabooed air, "Martin it's magnificent. A real masterpiece! This will be bigger than your mannequins!"

He ignored her, not hearing, not caring. The others remained silent. Just as well. They were irrelevant, all of them, except the priest who Martin had to try to make understand. This was between Martin and the image he conceived hidden in the light. The image that eluded him, which lay beyond his sight. Blood flowed to his cheeks. His heart pounded.

"Let's get some light on in here, Jimmy."

"Sure, Mr. Drake." Jimmy limped off, and soon the lights above them popped on in strings, bearing and then eating shadows as they lit.

Even in the light, the sculpture was fantastic. The others were confused by the spectacle of the master pacing before his miracle, creator of this creator, angry with his father/ child. Shocked by the bust that stirred their inner passion, they couldn't quite grasp the actions of the sculptor. There before beauty, Martin paced back and forth, fuming and clutching his hair in both hands, and glaring up at the sculpture they loved. Finally, sensing the battle in his friend, Father Manoel walked over to comfort him.

"Martin, it's magnificent. It's the most moving thing that I have ever seen."

"It's a failure," Martin spat, then turned to pace on, back and forth, more agitated than before.

Father Manoel followed him and soothed him, "Martin, you have done it! You've sculpted the face of God better than any other sculptor could have."

"Bull! An infant could do a better job with diaper shit."

"Martin, please."

The priest put a hand upon his shoulder, but Martin pulled away, then wheeled around and shouted, "What the fuck's the matter with you, Manoel? Don't you see what's wrong here? Aren't you supposed to be a holy man? What's wrong with this picture, Manoel? You tell me?"

Martin started circling the priest, who was bewildered by his unhappiness at such a great moment and by his mounting hostility.

"I don't know what's wrong, Martin. Please tell me."

"No, you tell me, Manoel. YOU TELL ME! You come barging up here, ripping my life apart, and making me feel like an asshole. Then you finally convince me that I can do the impossible, set me to the challenge and then sit there for a month watching me bust my balls with the effort. And now, when I fall flat on my ass in absolute failure, you're smiling and clapping like a baby in a candy store, too naive to realize what went wrong. What the fuck's the matter with you?"

"Martin, I don't understand..."

"Well, maybe you should try a little harder, goddamn it! No, you don't need to understand now. Do you? You got what you wanted—a suitcase full of money to take back to the kids! Forget about Martin. You got him all blown up full of self-belief, and now you abandon him on the eve of his great failure, taking the proof of it with you. I thought you were my friend."

Martin turned and walked away.

"Martin, I am your friend. I'll listen, so tell me what's wrong. Please."

The sculptor turned to face him. "Isn't it obvious?"

"No. No, it's not. Look, stop with your questions and tell me what's wrong. We'll fix it."

"There's no fixing it. It's done now, and it's wrong."

"What's wrong, Martin. Tell me."

The men walked to stand before the sculpture. The others stood behind them watching in silent amazement, Armine and Banks both amazed, but for different reasons.

"What are we looking at?" asked the sculptor, with less anger but with a growing impatience.

"It's your vision of the face of God."

"Right you are! And what does it tell you?"

"You show that even the most wonderful image man can create can't hold the essence of God."

"That's it, Manoel! That's the problem right there."

"But Martin, can't you see what you've done? You've shown the world that God is beyond our understanding, and you've done it with such skill and grace as to make your work a masterpiece."

"You still don't get it do you, Manoel?"

Martin's agitation was rising in quick crescendo.

"No, my friend, I'm afraid I don't."

226

"This bust is everything you just said—that's the point. The face I created is being blown apart by the inexplicable force within it. With this sculpture, I'm admitting failure. I didn't sculpt the face of God like you contracted me to do. I sculpted a clever fraud, a cute way to get out of giving you what you're paying for. I failed, Manoel. I failed."

Martin began pacing again.

Armine didn't like this shift to nonfulfillment of contractual obligations, so she strode to the artist to put an end to his tirade. She approached him and whispered quietly, "Enough with the tortured artist routine, Martin. Keep it up, and they'll start believing you. Calm down and start smiling!"

He ignored her, if he heard her, and turned back to the priest. Armine shrugged, popped on an apologetic smirk and clicked back over to Banks, who was intently watching the story playing out before him.

"Don't you see why I'm upset?" asked the artist to his friend. "I wanted so much to do something good after all of these years, and I put my blood in it. But for what? Nothing. I failed you, Manoel."

"Martin, you're being too hard on yourself. You always are. Of *course* you didn't capture the exact image of God. You can't. Nobody can. He's beyond us."

"But I can, Manoel. I can sculpt him if I can see him. I know it. I just need to see. Help me to see him."

"I will help you, Martin. I will, but I must tell you from what I see here, I think that maybe your vision's greater than mine."

"No! No, it's not. Don't you see—it's not."

Martin started pacing from the sculpture to the wall. The priest looked on, horrified at his friend's self-hate, and sorrowful for not knowing what to do about it. Martin paced to the wall again. Then on seeing a sledgehammer standing on its head below the catwalk, he grabbed it and rushed back to the work that caused him so much pain.

With a yell reminiscent to Father Manoel of Xingu Indians, Martin leaped to the statue and laid into it with several hard shots. Father Manoel ran to stop him, but before he could reach him, the damage was done. The Face of God was ravaged, gaping with wounds that revealed the light within to be nothing but a deceptive lamp. Tears welled in Father Manoel's eyes as he clutched his maddened friend. He pulled him away from the wreckage and threw the hammer down. They walked back to the others.

Martin composed himself and spoke calmly to Harry Banks. "Mr. Banks, I apologize. I wish you hadn't come here tonight and wasted your time. This wasn't what we were after. I see that now. I'll have something better for you in another three weeks. I still have time left."

Banks looked a long moment, appraising the sculptor before he spoke. "Mr. Drake, I don't know what kind of magic our good Father has worked on you, but I like it. I look forward to seeing your next statue and hope I can keep you from destroying it. You are an artist, Mr. Drake. I applaud you."

Banks shook Martin's hand. "You do realize, of course, that what expenses you've incurred here in your interesting creative process are yours to bear. The foundation can't be burdened with them."

"I don't care about the money, Mr. Banks. I just want to get it right."

"Yes, well. I believe you will, son. I believe you will."

Banks nodded to all of them and then headed for the door. Just before he reached it, he turned to call back. "Mr. Drake."

"Yes, sir?"

"You ought to know that if I hadn't already bought that bust, I would have offered you two million for it. Whether or not you cared for it, I thought it was magnificent. Maybe we can do more business in the future."

"I'd like that, Mr. Banks."

The billionaire departed. As soon as he was out of earshot, Armine turned upon the artist.

"Martin," she said. "You're right! Maybe I will give Vicki her own exhibition. She may be repulsive and obnoxious, but she would never throw away a million bucks. Get it together. I think you're losing your mind."

She clicked off quickly and slammed the door behind her as she left.

The sculptor turned to the foundryman, who had remained quiet through it all.

"Jimmy, I've got three weeks left. Can we make it?"

Jimmy rubbed his always aching hip and pondered the question, thinking of his crew and schedule. He looked up and answered, "Well, it will be a week at the plaster caster and at least another week here, not counting Sundays. I can't get anyone in on Sundays. We can do it, if you can get into plaster by the end of next week. Can you?"

"I can try."

"Well, then we'll see. But next time, do me a favor."

"Sure, Jimmy."

"Make sure you like the next one before I cast it. The boys and I put a lot of work in on this too, you know."

Martin nodded sheepishly. "Sorry Jimmy. I lost my head."

"Just get it right next time before you come to us, Martin. My old heart can't take the melodrama. Now, you two get out. I have to close shop. My wife's been complaining about these late hours. I may be ugly, but I warm the bed."

He grinned and swept them out to the parking lot.

The drive back to Manhattan was silent. Father Manoel was deep in thought. The future of his children was again in peril, but he wasn't thinking of that. He was wondering how he could help his friend find the vision he sought. He prayed for enlightenment and help as they drove.

Martin was also lost in thought. He was trying to overcome his frustration to concentrate on the question at hand. Who was God? What did he look like? He needed to know now, on this night. But still his mind was blank. The face he sought was hidden in the shadows of the years. He couldn't remember the last time he had prayed. Maybe that's what blocked him. Belief was first. The rest would follow.

The sculptor turned on to 15th Street still wondering, then pulled to a stop in front of the Lutheran Seafarer's House.

"Wake up, Manoel. We're here."

"I wasn't sleeping. I was praying."

"What about?"

"I was praying for God to guide you in your quest for inspiration, and I was asking for forgiveness for pushing you too hard."

"You didn't push me into anything, Manoel. I owe you a lot. If it wasn't for you, I'd be out somewhere tonight, prowling around, wasting what little of talent and life I still have. You gave it all back to me.

"I apologize for blowing up at you, Manoel. I can't explain it. This job has become big to me, bigger than anything since Sharon left me. I just want to do it right. I guess I took my frustration out on you because you're the only one who matters. I want to give you what you…what we decided on, and I knew that wasn't it. You know what, Manoel?"

"What's that, Martin?"

"It felt good smashing that thing. While he was there, I felt him looking at me, disappointed, but not now. I'm still all hyped up, but I feel better now that I have a fresh start. I really didn't want to see that statue roll out the door, and now I don't have to. One less worry." Traces of laughter bunched at the corners of Martin's red-ringed eyes, which then became contemplative.

"Manoel, what do you think God looks like?"

"I really don't know. I never thought much about it until you started this. For me, Christ on the crucifix was image enough. It doesn't matter. Belief and faith are what are important. All I can tell you is that the Book of Genesis teaches us that God created man in his own image. Maybe you should take a look in the mirror. He dwells in all of us."

The sculptor nodded.

"But don't think of that now. Get some rest. Will you please do that? You don't look good. I think you've been pushing yourself too hard on this. I don't want you to worry about me or my children. God will provide for us all. And unless I'm much mistaken, I think Harry Banks will underwrite us with or without your statue. So, please don't worry about anything other than settling yourself down. Relax and put your faith in the Lord. Pray for help. He answers prayers. And get some sleep tonight. You really don't look very good."

"I will. Thanks. Good night, my friend. I'll give you a call if I come up with something."

"There is one other thing I want to tell you, Martin, and maybe now's the time."

"Shoot, Manoel."

"Well, it's nothing really. It's just that I've been trying to think of some small way for us to pay you back for all the good you're doing for us. It's just a little thing, but I want you to know that we are naming one of our *crèches* after you. Harry Banks let me use his phone. I've already spoken to the board, and they've approved it."

"Thanks, Manoel!"

He was moved, and though Father Manoel couldn't see it, he blushed.

"That's nice," he said. "Maybe someday I'll come down to visit and teach the kids how to play with clay."

"I would like that, *meu amigo*. Now you go get some sleep."

Father Manoel gave Martin a bear hug, then opened his door and stepped out to the street. He closed the door, then hesitated at the curb. He turned around and knocked on the window. Martin lowered it.

"I picked this up before we left. I wanted it for me, but maybe it will help inspire you. It's a part of the most wonderful statue I have ever seen, except for Sharon, of course."

He handed Martin a shard of bronze, which had just been an eyebrow.

"Thanks, Manoel. Good night."

The priest smiled and walked away. Martin watched him make the door, where he stopped to wave before he entered. The sculptor waved back, then once Father Manoel was safe inside, he put his car in gear and headed uptown toward home.

Chapter Twenty-seven

MARTIN ENTERED HIS APARTMENT and walked right to the studio without bothering to change his clothes or even hang his coat. It was almost eleven. He hadn't slept well that afternoon while waiting for the bronze to cool. He had been too worried, too nervous, and he knew he couldn't sleep now—he had to come up with something and he was running out of time. He walked to his workbench and looked down at the lump of clay atop it, a shapeless remnant of his past failure. In his hand was the shard of bronze that Father Manoel had given him for inspiration. "Some inspiration," he scoffed, then tossed it on the bench beside the clay. He peeled off his coat, slung it across a chair and sat down to ponder the task before him, staring at the clay. It lay there lifeless, dead.

Slowly, Martin picked it up and tentatively shaped it in the form of a bust, like its many brethren he had summoned before. This noman faced him blank and empty, waiting for the promised spark in the sculptor's hands, but they faced an impasse. Nothing came. Nothing but an amassing frustration that blew upward from his spleen in a torrent of despair. He struck the form before him, pummeling it back into the mass from which it rose. It was gone, but his fury wasn't. He turned his hands on himself, striking himself again and again about the face and head. Harder and harder, he hit himself, but he couldn't dislodge the pain of failure that he hated himself for feeling.

"Goddamn you! Why can't you get it right? Why can't you? You can't do anything. You're fucking useless!"

He looked down again at the clay, and his savage anger grew. On seeing the glint of bronze beside it, his eyes widened, wild.

"Goddamn you!"

He clutched the bronze piece and beat it on his forehead, rapidly and as hard as he could. It's jagged edge scoured his flesh like a tiger paw and blood ran down his face, obscuring his vision with flowing, sticky heat. He let go. Bronze clattered to the floor, and he collapsed onto the workbench, sobbing and bleeding out his misery into the formless clay.

After a time, Martin's sobbing subsided as he tried to bring himself under control. He slowly picked himself up and looked around the room. On seeing Sharon, he stood up and approached. He softly stroked the cheek that shined from years of attention and gently wiped away her eternal tears while his ran freely. He bent to kiss her, then held onto her for support.

"I'm trying, sweetheart. I'm trying. You'd be proud. I'm working harder than I ever did...but I just can't seem to get it. I just can't see it."

He wiped away tears, and his hand came away with hot, tacky blood. He smiled. "I'm not much to look at, am I, sweet? Would you want me now, Sharon? You would, wouldn't you? God, I wish you hadn't had left. I wish I hadn't made you. Sharon, I was so bad to you. I was so stupid."

He caressed her hair and cheek with his bloodied hand, giving them the color that they had in life. Looking deep into her eyes of bronze that still cried the sad goodbye he had engraved in them, he remembered the happiness that had beamed through them during the years they had shared together. Their story played before him. He smiled and wished she were with him.

"You know the story of Pygmalion, sweet—the sculptor who carved a woman so perfect that he fell in love with her? I sometimes feel I'm him at night. I've often wished you'd come alive, turn around and come back to me. But you never did. I had my chance, my fair Galatea. I had my chance...."

He sadly watched her walk away—she was always walking away—then spoke again.

"You'd be happy if you knew what I was doing now, Sharon. You would. You should have seen the statue I destroyed today. It was magnificent, even better than you. It was the best thing I have ever done in my life, and I smashed it to bits because it wasn't good enough. You would have been so proud. And you should have seen Manoel's eyes, sweet—they were full of tears. He cried over my statue. He cried! It was that good. But not good enough. No, not good enough...

"I don't know if I can do this, baby, but I'm going to try until it kills me. If I could just see God for a moment, I know I could capture him in clay. I just need to see him. I just need to see."

He stroked her locks of bronze, then kissed her lips goodbye.

"Wish me luck, my sweet."

Martin turned to face his work and then slowly walked back to it.

When he sat down at his bench, he clutched the mound before him, drew it close and prayed for the first time in his memory. Blood and tears dripped down upon his earthy altar.

"God, please help me to see you. Let me do this right. Forgive me my wasted years and squandered talent. Help me with this. Give this to me, so that I can give it to Manoel and to the world. Let me see you. Please..."

His hesitant prayer came easier than he thought it would, and a peace that he had never felt before poured through him. Maybe Father Manoel was right: God does dwell in each of us. Martin could feel God then. He smiled in joy and relief. He finally understood!

In a rush, he was once again at work. His flurried hands molded the clay up into the too familiar shape—a faceless bust awaiting its identity, and this time Martin had one to give it. He worked as if possessed, seeming not to see the clay but instead to see inside it. As he formed the key to unlock the holy mystery, he swelled with boundless joy that threatened to burst his already aching heart with shudders that shot through his chest down to his kneading, painful fingers. This was it. He knew it. His heart pounded in his temples, which burned with concentrated light. He sweat into the cool wintered studio in waves of anticipation.

Hours passed unheeded. The moon, once visible, arced beyond the skylights and was gradually replaced by the pink and purple promise of the coming dawn. Martin worked on, oblivious, enraptured, stopping only for the odd moment to sit back for quick inspections, which were acted upon with expert dabs and tucks from knowing fingers that smudged away a ridge here, reworked an eyebrow there. And then finally, with the ruddy reds and oranges that heralded the day, after his ultimate, critical assault, it was done.

Martin sat back and stared down at his creation with wide, believing eyes. His joy spilled freely down his face, and he shuddered with an ecstasy beyond the pain that gripped him, and which wouldn't let him breathe.

Etched with the beauty and wisdom of the ages, glowing with a power beyond the realm of understanding, it was he himself that stared back. It was God crying the mirrored tears of the sculptor, welcoming home the prodigal son, once lost but now returned triumphant. Martin, moved, reached out to hug his father, and they were reunited, even as his body slumped and as his face crushed down to bury itself in his lost creation.

The first rays of morning sun poured into the studio in a warming flight, shining down upon Martin's body and glinting back from Sharon, who now smiled.

-The End-

Cited Works

Blake, William. "The Garden of Love." *The Illuminated Blake: William Blake's Complete Illuminated Works with a Plate-by-Plate Commentary,* edited by David V. Erdman, Dover, 1971, plate. Songs 441.

Jastrow, M., Gotthell, G. "Rock of Ages." *Armed Forces Hymnal,* US Government Printing Office, p. 111.

Whiting, William. "Eternal Father Strong to Save." *Armed Forces Hymnal,* US Government Printing Office, p. 390.

Notes and Acknowledgments

T HIS IS A WORK of fiction, and all of its characters are fictitious. Orlando Villas Boas and his brothers, Leonardo and Claudio, were historical figures who did much to protect and preserve the Xingu Indians. They were pivotal in helping to establish the Xingu Indigenous Park in 1961. To my knowledge, the Villas Boas brothers never employed missionaries in their work, but missionaries have been active in the Xingu since the 1960s. The Txukarramãe and the Suyá are real tribes that inhabit the Xingu, and Orlando Villas Boas was the first to make peaceful contact with them. The Txukarramãe had a violent history in relation to encroachment on their lands until the early 1980s, but as their territorial boundaries are no longer in dispute, they have been mostly peaceful since. The Suyá were decimated by a series of measles epidemics, but have staged a comeback. They numbered 127 in a census taken in 1982. Another tribe, the Tsuvá, were not so lucky and became extinct through measles in 1954. Measles and other diseases have been plagues to Xingu Indians and were passed to them by government employees or missionaries who worked on their behalf.

The work of Father Manoel is loosely based on that of my dear friend, Dona Alberta Gasparini, 'Vó Tina,' who founded the *'Instituto Caminho de Luz'* near Brasília-DF, Brazil. The character of Manoel himself is loosely based on another good friend, Padre Samuel Ferreira do Carmo, SVD.

I thank Laurie Dove for her skilled editing, and I thank Zach Hunter and the production team at Goldtouch Press for their effort in bringing this book to market.

Finally, I would like to give very special thanks to my wife, Silviane Tusi Brewer, for her constant support and advice.